THE ART OF TOMB RAIDING

AHIMSA KERP

SEVEREDPRESS

THE ART OF TOMB RAIDING

WWW.SEVEREDPRESS.COM

This novel is a work of fiction. Names, characters, places and incidents are the product of the author's imagination, or are used fictitiously. Any resemblance to actual events, locales or persons, living or dead, is purely coincidental.

ISBN: 978-1-923165-60-1

"To awaken quite alone in a strange town is one of the most pleasant sensations in the world. You are surrounded by adventure. You have no idea of what is in store for you, but you will, if you are wise and know the art of travel, let yourself go on the stream of the unknown and accept whatever comes in the spirit in which the gods may offer it. For this reason your customary thoughts, all except the rarest of your friends, even most of your luggage - everything, in fact, which belongs to your everyday life, is merely a hindrance...[I]f you discard all this, and sally forth with a leisurely and blank mind, there is no knowing what may not happen to you."
— Freya Stark

Special thanks to early readers and givers of feedback Janessa PK, Wind Lothamer, Garrett Calcaterra, and Ieva Rute

PROLOGUE

I always liked my Uncle Jad, although I never got to see much of him. When he died I was in my first year of uni at La Trobe University in Victoria. I was sad but I was so busy that I didn't have time to process it and then second year came, I joined the newspaper, got a girlfriend, and I admit that I kind of forgot about him. I had a new life and it wasn't until I came home the summer after I graduated that I allowed those old feelings to finally be unpacked.

My mum had given me a large box he left with my name on it. They were things he had collected, odd tchotchkes from around the world. I was at an age where I didn't really appreciate the silver bracelets from Morocco, the Kenyan beaded necklaces, the decorative tiles from Spain, traditional Japanese sake cups, sarongs from India, Persian saffron, batiks from Borneo, Buddhist statues from Thailand and Laos, tons of random coins and colorful banknotes, and of course faded postcards with a vast array of landmarks, natural wonders, and cityscapes from around the world. Uncle Jad had been a traveler, a collector, and, he would have once said, a tomb raider, although he would have complained that a certain video game character ruined that term for him.

I did get lost in thought, thinking of all those trips, all those experiences, all that world seen and lost. But I didn't look much at it until once I twisted at a beaded necklace from Bangladesh and it came apart. I thought I had broken it but then I looked closer. There was a USB port attached to the large turquoise bead. Bemused, I opened up my backpack and pulled out my laptop. I plugged the USB in and saw a prompt for the password. There was room for six characters, but whether they were numbers or letters or symbols I had no idea. I almost gave up but then I thought: he left this *for me*. He must have thought I could do this.

I wasn't sure how many tries I had and I worried that it could be a one-and-done kind of deal. It was at least easy to rule some things out. Uncle Jad was paranoid and it would not be our birth dates, or one of our names. It would never be anything so simple. I might have sighed once or twice in frustration. I had just finished finals and my brain was at low power. Even simple tasks were a challenge. I was again about to pull out the USB and box up the world's treasures for perhaps the last time when I saw it. The bead had just the sketch of a face. Oval eyes and a smear of a mouth. Six letters. The birthday of our shared favorite actor, the man who had died too soon. We celebrated every 4th of April by watching a

Heath Ledger movie. I typed in 040479. The USB opened. There was only one file there, a word doc with the title “Zoroastrianism and the Art of Tomb Raiding.” That was Uncle Jad's humor. I was sitting cross-legged in the attic. As I read through the document, the afternoon passed outside. Evening came and went. Mum and Dad came home from work, cooked dinner, ate dinner, washed the dishes, watched tv, and went to bed. Probably they looked for me but I could not be found. I sat there unmoving in the attic, utterly transfixed by the story before my eyes. By the time I finished, it was past midnight, my legs ached, and I really had to go pee.

Only later, as I played back certain scenes in my head would I wonder why there was so much secrecy. I could have easily never found that USB, though it was clearly left for me and me alone. I mean, it had taken me over four years to find it.

How much of the story is actually true? That is up to you to decide. I know for a fact that some things happened but there are parts of this tale that stretch credulity and some must be fiction. I refused to believe many parts of Uncle Jad’s story but as time has passed I’m not sure.

I present to you the story I found, supplemented by myself to add information where I thought it needed. I have mostly kept the title the same, and that is the most significant change I made. I have done little other than arrange his long manuscript into chapters. Every once in a while, when something was out of order, I moved it to make the narrative more clear. Some parts are missing but it’s nothing too important. I also cleaned up some of the language. Uncle Jad was of the generation that thought little of using the hated “See You Next Tuesday” word. In lieu of that particular epithet, I have substituted the phrase “unpleasant person” but you’ll know what he meant. So without further ado, I present to you the impossible story that could possibly be true.

Ahimsa Kerp

1

G'day. I reckon I've told this story, or at least parts of it, dozens of times. But until now I've never dared to tell the entire truth. It irked me, don't get me wrong. A guy like me lives on reputation as much as anything, and without words or language there is no such thing as reputation. There is no such thing as me. So consider this a confessional. I almost said "deathbed" but (knock on wood) I'll be around for quite a long time. Well, enough faffing about. Let's get started.

Some sights are so singular, so beautiful that to see them is to experience profound regret, for you instinctively know that nothing in your life, long as it may be, will ever equal it. If you're wondering if you have ever seen such a thing, you haven't. You'll know when you do. And it makes all the pain, the loss, the hurt … well, not worth it, not exactly, but more acceptable. It recontextualizes everything that led up to it.

I'm faffing about again. Look, this story started on a blistering hot January day in Melbourne. The city was just stuffed up with people in for the Australian Open. I couldn't give a flying damn about tennis but the city has a certain vibe about it. I run (ran maybe) a little curio shop named Get Lost! on Little Collins Street. I sell maps, jigsaw puzzles, vintage tea towels, taxidermized critters, whatever tack I can get my hands on and pass off to tourists on the search for something "authentic." *Where's somewhere authentic we can eat at?* I get asked twice a day. The big Seppos, whinging Poms, even the bloody French. The expectant look in their eyes, mate. As if I am going to tell them about a kangaroo steak place that only locals go to. They laugh when I tell them to go to Hungry Jack's or some such hamburger joint, and I laugh too, but I'm not joking.

You get so you can recognize people when they come in. The ones wasting time, the ones who want to drop some dough on this trinket or that bauble. This bloke, I knew he was trouble but I couldn't place him. He wasn't from here, but wasn't European, didn't look Middle-eastern or Hispanic. He wore a designer suit, polished shoes, the kind of sunnies that showed me myself better than it showed him.

He said he had something to sell. "Mate," I said. "Mate, you got it backwards. I sell all the rubbish you see in here. You give me money for them. That's how it works." His English was good, but his accent was hard to place. Not Persian, not Russian. But something not a million miles away from either of those.

He pulled out a map. There was something about it. It was like the document was charged with energy that I could feel but not see. The hairs on the back of my neck rose, and that's not just an expression. They really stood up in a thrillingly unpleasant way.

He knew, somehow, what seeing the map would do to me. He held it up for me to see briefly. There were topographical details that excited me with their mute promise of discovery and adventure.

"I'm listening," I said, trying to sound casual. My voice was slightly thick with repressed emotion and this man did not fail to notice it.

He proceeded to tell me a tale that involved a ticket to St. Kilda, a bus ticket to Healesville Sanctuary, a metal comb, a packet of gum, an empty vape pen and so on. I recognized the details. This was the story of The Somerton Man, updated regionally and temporally. That was one of the great mysteries of Australia. Did this cheeky bugger really not expect me to know that? Thing is, though, it didn't matter what he said. I wanted that map and I didn't care about the free lies that came with it.

"Yeah, alright," I said casually when he finished. "I might have a place for such a thing."

The dance began. Neither of us wanted to name a price, and we went back and forth for a while. I remember he was nervous. I couldn't see his eyes behind those reflective shades, but he glanced back at the door more than once. He gave in at last and named a price that made my eyes water and arse clench. We bickered and I ended up dropping a lot of moolah. How much? Let's just say I could have had a nice used car instead. But that bloody map had cast a bloody spell on me. Besides, it was an investment. That's what I told myself. I might not find a real treasure, but I could at least flip it for something more.

The bloke took the money and left with nary another word. I was cranky that afternoon about the dosh I'd dropped, but that poor bugger would be dead before the next day and I was about to leave the country to find the greatest thing ever discovered, so looking back, yeah, I could have been in a better mood.

I glanced at the map but I knew I needed to savor it. There was writing in Cyrillic on it and I recognized one word. Kavkaz. But I stopped reading after that. This was a present I needed to wait until exactly the right time to unwrap.

I had no idea yet, but my life had changed. Utterly and incontrovertibly. I had plans that night to meet a few mates out at a little brewpub in Fitzroy. I already knew the beer I wanted to try too: a nice hoppy IPA. I know that's kind of a wanker beer but you like what you like, and I've always loved the stuff. I fancied one of the girls that was going to be there and I had just finished a Colleen Hoover book I read specifically to impress her.

The assassin changed all that.

2

I haven't exactly lived what you would call a normal life: there have been plenty of brushes with danger. In 2016, I spent nine days in an Uzbek jail (for taking photos of the subway, believe it or not). As a younger man, I got lost in the Amazon for five-and-a-half weeks and by the time I emerged, I had more leeches than body fat. Just last year I went crocodile hunting in the Sepik Valley, which, let me tell you, is *not* for the faint hearted. I still have scars and nightmares. But nothing had prepared me for the eventuality of another person trying to take my life away from me.

That said, I wasn't *that* surprised either. For someone in my line of work, a bloke who acquires a lot of rare artifacts, it's always kind of in the back of your mind. So after I closed up shop and headed to the tram, I clocked the unpleasant person right away. Looked like an American tourist: white socks, white trainers, Yankees baseball cap. That alone wouldn't have piqued my interest, but he started walking towards me in a very deliberate manner. His hand was in the pocket of his blue jumper but his elbow jutted out at a dangerous angle. Suddenly he was there, right in front of me.

It was an out-of-body experience. There were people all around us, flowing past me in either direction but only this Yank tourist existed. Something silver flashed as his hand withdrew. A blade came at my gut, hoping to spill me open like a Christmas cracker. But my survival instincts kicked in and I pushed his arm down whilst leaping away. The blade went skittering away into the gutter. Did anyone notice? Hard to imagine they didn't, but no one said anything or reacted. People are pretty jaded these days, or assume it's some kind of TikTok challenge.

The Yank was a pro. His attempt thwarted, he cut his losses and moved past me into the crowd. I had been so focused on the threat of the blade, I'd barely seen his face. He looked like any white guy in his 30s. Sharp features. Mustache. Broad shoulders. He could have been anyone, but there was something unsettling about him. Was he wearing a mask?

My heart was pounding as my brain just started to process what had happened. I tried to tell myself that it wasn't about the map but nothing else made sense. The only surprising thing was how quickly they had gotten onto me. They must have been following the guy who sold it to me, ready to pounce on him. He had dispersed with the cursed item just in time. That meant that this map was really valuable. Too valuable. That worried me. But also I had to wonder who "they" were. Already I suspected some organization. This was a professional, a hired gun who worked for other people.

I don't remember getting on the tram, or riding it, though I surely did both those things. I had to assume that the would-be assassin would be back. Even if I could evade him, others would come in his place. I couldn't afford to think otherwise. I keep a low profile online, other than the shop, so I felt safe in that regard. I could go home, book a flight, and at least get a head start on this map business.

I got off the tram on Wright Street. It was a random stop but I had realized I couldn't go out to meet my mates. It could put them in danger. My whole life had changed. I took a deep breath as I began to contemplate the steep cliff I teetered on. You might wonder why I didn't get rid of the map, or at least consider it as an option. The truth is that it didn't even occur to me. It already had that much of a hold on me. The fact that they had tried to kill me without even making an offer to buy it was chilling. For someone, knowledge of this map was considered a capital offense.

Three other people had gotten off with me but they went separate directions as I began to walk back to the north. This whole time I had tried not to give myself away, but now my hand reached to my inner chest pocket. The map was still there. It had to be, but still, it was good to know. I could feel the coarse texture of the old paper. It was almost fuzzy. I glanced behind me to make sure no one was following me and set off.

I wandered aimlessly, lost in a daze of paranoia. Except are you actually paranoid if someone tried to kill you that very day? I walked for some time (an hour? two?) before I reached the Swanston line. This would take me out to where I stayed out toward East Malvern. Feeling a bit ridiculous, I looked behind me. Nobody was following me.

My mind slowly returned and I began to calm down. I checked my phone and saw that Dante had SMSed me several times. I hadn't remembered to tell them I wasn't coming. I messaged back, using the word beetroot. We had a root vegetable code. If you mentioned one, it meant trouble. The bigger the veg, the bigger the trouble.

Dante messaged me back right away. "Get your burger without beetroot next time, mate." This was an offering of help. I considered it for a moment, but dismissed it quickly.

"Good idea. I will let you know." This wasn't code so much as me waffling in indecision. I wasn't saying "yes" to help, but I wasn't saying "no" either. I needed time to think. A few minutes later, I quickly swiped out a follow-up message. "Might be jetting out soon. Fancy a trip?"

There was no response and I was left unread. Knowing Dante, he had probably replaced the phone with a schooner of ale. That was fine. It gave me time to think, which I did, and then I was almost home.

3

Hi, it's me, the nephew, here. Uncle Jad didn't say much about the assassin, obviously, because at the time he didn't know who it was. But I've done some research, delved into the dark web, made some inquiries and now have a good idea. It's chilling to consider. Here's what I found out.

Dossier on "The Raven"

Age: Estimated to be in their mid-30s to early 40s.

Nationality: Unknown, with potential ties to the British Isles or North America, though their exact origin is unconfirmed.

Background: The assassin known only as "The Raven" has been active in covert operations for over a decade, though rumors of their exploits suggest a far longer career. Their true identity remains shrouded in secrecy. Interpol, CIA, and MI6 have all opened case files on this individual, but no one has ever come close to apprehending or even identifying them. "The Raven" is known for their meticulous planning, high-level strategic thinking, and an uncanny ability to disappear without a trace after completing a job.

Modus Operandi: Unlike most assassins who specialize in a particular method, "The Raven" is a master of all forms of killing. They have been linked to deaths by poison, sniper fire, car explosions, hand-to-hand combat, and even elaborate accidents. This versatility makes them highly unpredictable and adaptable to any environment. "The Raven" has a preference for psychological manipulation, often creating elaborate traps or misleading law enforcement to believe the death was a suicide, natural causes, or the work of another group.

Training: It is widely believed that "The Raven" has undergone some of the most advanced military training available. Some intelligence reports suggest they may have been a former special forces operative, potentially linked to Sayeret Matkal, the Israeli elite special forces. Their proficiency in close-quarters combat, long-range shooting, and survival in hostile environments indicates training that far exceeds that of ordinary mercenaries or criminals. Several of their assassinations have involved deep infiltration into highly secure locations, hinting at espionage-level skills in surveillance, hacking, and lockpicking.

Psychological Profile: Psychological profiling of "The Raven" suggests an individual with extreme intelligence, patience, and control over their emotions. Unlike other contract killers who may seek notoriety or wealth, "The Raven" is a ghost. They operate without ego, leaving no room for error, and their actions appear to be guided by a deep, possibly pathological sense of duty or vendetta. Experts have debated whether they are a sociopath or psychopath, but one thing is clear: "The Raven" feels no remorse, no guilt. They kill without hesitation, often manipulating the emotional states of their targets beforehand, showing an unnerving capacity for cruelty.

Notable Contracts: Several high-profile assassinations have been attributed to "The Raven," though direct evidence remains elusive. These include the death of a Russian oligarch in London, the suspicious crash of a private jet carrying several heads of state, and the poisoning of a high-ranking intelligence officer in Berlin. Rumor has it that "The Raven" has also conducted assassinations on behalf of rogue states, private military contractors, and clandestine organizations, further complicating any attempts to track their movements.

Network and Resources: "The Raven" does not appear to work alone. While their network remains hidden, intelligence suggests they have access to a global web of informants, safe houses, and weapons caches. Their ability to cross borders undetected, acquire cutting-edge technology, and gather intelligence on targets is beyond the scope of any ordinary operator. Some speculate that "The Raven" is sponsored by a shadow government or private entity with vast resources. Alternatively, they may operate through a loose collection of mercenaries, hackers, and corrupt officials who owe them favors or share similar goals.

All of that is terrifying to think of. A deadly assassin coming after my uncle. But the true horror, as I learned and as you will learn, comes from the entity that hired him. And who he really turned out to be.

4

My house is nothing special. Everyone says Malvern is for poshos and it's true that you have to have some money to live out here. But I've never believed in investing in the place where you sleep, the same way I don't waste money on plush bog roll. Yeah I can afford it, but not when there are so many more interesting things to spend your hard-earned cash on. I still remember the ad written on the realtor's website. Something like: "Featuring a charming brick exterior with a classic red-tiled roof and curved awnings over the windows. A neat front yard with a grassy lawn and a tree creates a welcoming atmosphere. The facade is simple yet elegant, with two large windows to the left. Next to it is a single-car garage with a white door. This home exudes a cozy, suburban feel." Just the most boring place. So yeah, my home is not the mansion you might expect, despite the million plus dollar price tag. But the stuff on the inside? Priceless.

I paused at the door and then slowly opened it. The only warning I had was that my house was trashed. Magazines were strewn about all over the place. The statue of the wolf I had picked up in Killin, Scotland, had been overturned. The sofa was ripped to pieces. I thought I heard a noise from the back but I didn't wait around to confirm. I quickly closed the door and locked it again. Then I turned and ran.

Part of me, a little nugget of consciousness hidden beneath my terror, felt ridiculous. Was it an overreaction? This was fucked. How had they tracked me down? It had only been a few hours and what kind of resources could they bring to bear to have tracked *me* down. Who, in a word, were *they*?

I turned a corner and ducked into a small park. A few children played at their parent's feet, but the slide and the swings were empty. I sat on one of the swings and pulled out my phone.

I didn't text Dante. He might not look for hours. I texted Nova instead. She would be next to Dante, and she checked her phone a bit more than he did. "Going to get dinner, maybe some parsnip for the barbie." It didn't matter what I wrote, so long as I included a root vegetable.

She answered back almost instantly. My phone buzzed in my hand but I glanced around. A woman playing with her child in the grass. A couple of other kids playing tag. A black car drove by on the street. It was driving slowly, but was it driving too slowly? I looked back at my phone as casually as I could. Nova had written simply, "Sure. Where?"

"Meet at Mel's," I responded and put my phone away. This was simple code. MEL was Tullamarine Airport. I was getting out of dodge and it didn't matter that I was going the most obvious way, perhaps even the way I was being driven. I had a few tricks up my sleeve, you see.

I sat on the swing and took a deep breath. I was ready to leap up and escape but it was then I began to shake. The events of the last couple of hours, beginning with the knife assailant and ending with my home being raided, hit me. I had a hard time breathing and suddenly I felt like I might vomit. I put my head down into my hands and breathed slowly while mentally digging myself out the hole I suddenly found myself in.

It was only for a moment but I felt a little better. When I looked up, the black car had stopped on the edge of the park. I couldn't see who was in it but it gave me a really bad feeling. The two mums and their babies didn't look up. I slowly stood up and walked over to one of them.

She was 30ish, had curly dark hair and an assertive nose. Sitting on a bench above a two year old playing with a wooden duck in the grass, she looked at me warily as I approached, as well she might. I was in a tricky position. I wanted it to appear to any would-be observers that this was my family. I wasn't some solo guy that would be easy to kill. I was a father with my kids at the park. But I also had to convince this woman to speak to me, that I was no danger.

I started in safe territory. "Shit weather lately, eh?"

She did not relax, just nodded as she looked at me expectantly. Her eyes spoke clearly to me: *what do you want*? I stood there awkwardly, then sat down beside her. She stiffened.

I couldn't think of any lie desperate enough to convince her to speak with me, so I tried something even more dangerous. The truth.

"Look, I'm sorry to bother you. But there's some people following me. Don't look. But there's a black car over there. Don't look! Just nod if you saw it before."

She nodded slowly.

"I don't know what they want, but they're up to no good. If you let me sit here for a minute, I'll go soon."

She glanced down to her little ankle-biter and again I could hear her thoughts. "It's no danger to you or the sprog," I said, gesturing down at the little one. "I promise." I hoped I could promise that. Truly, I was that desperate, though I am not proud of it.

"I live in the area," I said, talking to her to soothe her, like one might with a wild cat. "Been here for six, seven years? Maybe you've seen me riding my bike around. I work in the CBD, have a little shop. Get Lost! on Collins Street."

This did seem to relax her a bit. That's a rather flash area, if I do say so myself. The slope of her shoulders sagged a bit and she seemed to lose the nervous tension that had filled her. She no longer looked like she was about to spring away. Over her shoulder, the black car slowly reversed and then drove away. I watched it for a moment, until it was out of sight.

"Thank you," I said, rising to my feet. "I appreciated our chat."

"I didn't even say a word," she said.

I paused for a moment, playing back what had happened. She was right. I then shrugged and gave her a wave. She'd have a strange story to tell and I would live to fight another day. Whether that car had really been looking for me or not, I couldn't know, but I certainly had to operate as though it had been.

It would be nice to return home and collect my passport, some cash, and a few travel necessities. But I couldn't do that, certainly not any time soon. Maybe not ever again. The first rule in tomb raiding: always have your bug out bag ready and hidden somewhere only you can find it. It's better to have more than one (I will admit to having at least six here in Melbourne) but at a minimum you need the one. So I caught a cab, picked up my bag (no, I will not tell you from where) and an hour later I was at the airport.

5

I picked up my trusty Macpac at a storage locker in the airport. It had been everywhere with me (literally all seven continents) and was currently filled with clothing, books, and freeze-dried food. I had bought this pack ten years ago in Christchurch New Zealand and it was still nearly as good as new. The Kiwis knew a thing or two about trekking, even if they called it by the wrong name. I felt good, ready to go, and so I hoofed it to Hungry Jack's to meet Nova and Dante. The food smelled good so I grabbed some thick cut chips and got a table. Placing my back to the wall, I ripped out a page of my journal and scribbled seven words on it, then tucked it into my pocket. I had positioned myself so I could browse the crowd.

I saw Nova first. Nova Wilder. The name fit, for there were few more wild than she. Her dark curly hair cascaded down her head, giving her the appearance of a lion. Tall for a woman, and broad-shouldered, she looked like an athlete but in truth was one of the least coordinated, most unco people I have ever known. She was wearing her bright orange vest, the one with a dozen or more pockets because of course she was. I don't think I've ever seen her without it.

Dante Merriweather, true to form, was drunker than a poet on payday. He could not resist an airport lounge beer or six. And to be fair, they had come straight from the pub. He was tall, as close to two meters as it didn't make a difference and not fat, not thin, just normal sized. His legs were long though, and his torso small. His arms were quite short for his height and he could not reach all of his back. He buzzed his hair to the scalp except for a bit of a mohawk that sat uneasily on the top of his head like a cat stuck in a tree. Though he enjoyed laughing and playing pranks upon occasion, he had a severe case of resting unpleasant person face. He looked like what he was: a dude you did not want to fuck with.

"Hi," he said, extending his big mitt of a hand. "I'm Dante Merriweather. Pleased to meet ya'."

"Fuck you," I said, laughing. One of my biggest flaws is that when I ask someone their name, I forget to listen to what their name actually is. I had to ask Dante four different times before his name stuck. He likes to remind me of this, every now and again.

"What's up, boss?" Nova asked. Her eyes never rested as they took in all of the airport around us.

You might think that standing in the middle of a public space is a bad place to exchange secrets, and if so you're not wrong. But there was safety in the anonymity of the crowd too. We walked nowhere in particular and spoke in low voices as I explained the situation to them.

"I bought something today. Within the hour, someone tried to kill me. When I got home, my house had been tossed. Pros. They were there when I came in and almost made me a little later."

Both of my companions were veterans but neither could hide their look of surprise.

"Heavy shit, boss," Nova said.

"Interesting," Dante said.

"I've got to make tracks," I told them. "Destination: unknown."

"Mind if I ask what you bought?" Nova asked.

There was no reason not to tell them. In fact, I needed to let them know. Our healthy relationship was based as much on my respect for them as it was the money I paid them. But I felt a strange reluctance to talk about it. "A map," I said at last. "I've not even had a chance to look at it much, but I think it's in a former Soviet Republic."

Dante shook his head. "Oh no. I'm not going back to Almaty. Twice was enough."

"You're not going anywhere, mate," I told him. "Not yet. I need some gear you can collect and then come meet us."

He nodded at that.

I turned to Nova as she subtly scanned the baggage area, the large crowd of French tourists walking by, and the juice kiosk in the corner. Was that woman with the green smoothie watching us too closely? Or was her obvious interest a trap? I shook my head to disperse the clouds of paranoia and focused on Nova's dark green eyes.

"What do you say? You ready for a trip?"

Her eyes met mine for just a moment. "Well I worked all day, had a few beers, was planning on watching a kung fu flick tonight, and I don't know where you're going."

I waited. She had a flair for the dramatic.

"In other words," she said. "Yeah. Let's do it."

I handed Dante the ripped out notebook page. He scanned it and when he saw the last two words, he looked surprised for the second time that night.

"Does that really say…?" he asked.

"Yup," I said.

"Where am I going to…? Alright, alright. I'll sort it out."

"I knew you would."

He was already turning away.

"Dante," I called. "Be careful."

He turned back. "It's easy for me," he said as he strode away out of the airport. I watched him exit and then turned to her. Nova said nothing but her eyes were a pool of questions.

I reached into my airport bag and tossed her a passport.

6

I never sleep on planes. I'm too tall, for one, and I refuse to sleep in public. Of course, this time I fell asleep immediately. Once I was able to relax, I fully relaxed. I only woke up when the cabin bell dinged and the pilot announced we'd shortly be reaching our destination and the temperature was 26 degrees Celsius.

That layover, three days in Kuala Lumpur, is hazy as I try to think about it now. So too is the bus ride to Singapore, the flight to Mumbai, the bus/train/bus to Delhi, and then the trek into the Thar Desert. But I won't ever forget the discussion I had with Nova on that first leg of the flight.

She had watched me while I was sleeping. As the lights came back on we started talking about things, in a way we hadn't for a long time. I think she sensed my fear and in her way she tried to help. "So, my mate plays a lot of poker. Me personally, I hold onto things, people, jobs, ideas for too long. But he, you know, he knows when to hold them and when to fold them."

Her description of herself did not match my own impression of her, not by a long shot. But I said nothing as the stewardess came by and asked the man in front of us to put his tray down. Nova continued in a low, urgent whisper.

"Poker has a lot of analogies to life, and this is what I've learned from playing with him. Sometimes an expert player will fold with an incredible hand. That is called the hero fold, and it is the hardest one. You will never know if you made the right decision or not. You can agonize forever, dwelling on it. But the point is you make your best move and then you move on to the next hand."

"Why are you telling me this?"

She looked slightly annoyed at the interruption and then finished her speech.

"Closure doesn't come from knowing if you were going to win or going to lose. You'll never know, not in poker, not in life. Most people don't show their cards, not in life and not in poker. You just have to trust that you made the best decision with the information you had. Remember: you can't always get what you want," she sang.

I looked at her silently as the plane came to a bumpy landing. I understood the point she was making, but not why. But I knew she wouldn't tell me more. This was for me to figure out. She let me have the time to process. She was truly an incredible person.

7

"Do you like Pakistan?"

I once heard a thumbs up described to me by my nephew as "the way that very old people posed for photos." Guilty as charged, I suppose. I do indeed rely on the thumbs up when taking photos. But for me those thumbs will always mean hitchhiking. If it wasn't before we entered Pakistan, it would be forever more after that. We were officially thumb riders.

"Do you like Pakistan?"

I had last written that we had entered the Thar Desert. When you think of the part of India that is camels lumbering over sand dunes, that is where you are thinking of. It is located in Rajasthan, a place that maintained its independence for hundreds of years through a series of powerful lords (rajas) nestled in powerful fortresses. Nova had spent some time here, but a guide was not needed. The Rajastani people were hospitable and kind. We even met a magnificently mustachioed man who had been voted "Mr Rajasthan" for three years straight (he confided to us that the award was given mostly on a facial hair basis.)

"Do you like Pakistan?"

We fended off various would-be guides, including a man who followed us around telling us questionable facts ("children in the desert city of Jaisalmer will often grow to seven years old without ever seeing rain") and eventually rented camels for ourselves. I don't know if you have ever ridden a camel, but it's the only way to travel. So much smoother than a horse. We rode out for a couple of days to an old Hindu temple where, strangely, the only food they had was instant ramen. Perhaps just as strange, it was served by young men in the Indian Army, because we were so close to the border. A little baksheesh got us into Pakistan with no fuss, no muss.

It was here, now that we had ditched our camels and stuck out our thumbs, that the questions started. "Do you like Pakistan?" It's a question all the people we met liked to ask after "Which country?" "What is your job?" and "Is she your girlfriend?" I provided various answers to the askers of these questions, the various fruit sellers, shoe shiners, kids on bikes, rickshaw drivers, blokes in giant trucks, but I always said Nova was my girlfriend, or my wife if they asked that. It was too hard to explain that a man and woman might be together and not romantically inclined. They liked her green eyes and commented endlessly upon them. She, an experienced traveler in these countries, even found a ring for sale in a dusty market and wore it. I didn't have its twin but for some reason no one ever looked at my hand.

We sat on our rucksacks on the back of a bouncing four wheeler on our way to a town called Kashmore. Our plan was to get a bus from there to Islamabad, then rent motorcycles and drive up the Karakoram Highway and ultimately end up in the Kumrat Valley. That would be one of the safest places to lie low in the world, not to mention one of the most scenic. Like most good plans, this was never going to happen but we didn't know that yet.

This was when our shithouse truck stopped to allow a man on. Our new companion, a young man struggling with seven feisty chickens, was dressed in a dusty, mustard-yellow tank top, and had a pencil thin mustache that would not have impressed anyone in Rajasthan. His eyes were a startling shade of blue. He spoke only to me, even when Nova addressed him.

"Where are you from?"

I sometimes lied in answer to this question. Many touts and salesmen use it to establish a relationship, and indeed they have memorized the capital cities, leaders, and populations of almost every country in the world. To forestall this, I usually told them I was from Latveria, which made them think long enough for me to walk past. But in this case I told him the truth.

"I'm from Australia, mate."

"Australia?" he said. "Kangaroos!"

"Yup, that's right," I said. That was a typical response, although sometimes the animal they referenced was koalas.

"Do you like Pakistan?" he asked.

"We've only just got here," Nova said politely. I stared at the unchanging landscape as we went over another bump.

The man nodded at her answer, waited a few seconds, and then repeated his question to me.

Nova sighed and glanced at me. It was my turn and I knew the answer.

"Yes I love it here. The food, the mountains, such a great cricket team, and most of all the wonderful people."

"The people here are so kind," Nova chimed in.

The man smiled broadly even as he clutched a squirming chicken to his chest. "Thank you," he said.

You might think I'd feel bad. In my defense, I do feel bad that I didn't feel bad. But the truth is, I was so used to manipulating people, telling them what they wanted to hear, that I didn't even think about it.

To me, the man was just another obstacle to overcome, another hazard of the trip.

"Come to dinner with me and my family," he said. "I cook." He hefted the squirming chicken to make it clear what would be on the menu and I suddenly had empathy for the struggling foul.

"My wife and I would love to," I said. My eyes met Nova's own green ones with an amused expression as I said this. "But we have far to go today."

"Thank you," she said. "Maybe next time." That phrase was a golden ticket to escape obligation across Asia. Ironic, really, since it was just a polite way of saying no. Like any good magical phrase, it worked perfectly.

The man nodded gratefully, displaying a huge smile. Then the truck hit a bump and the rogue chicken slipped from his grasp. He bent to collect it again and another escaped from the sack. I stood up to possibly help him, or at least to let him know that I was willing to, but he waved me away as a large truck rushed by in the other lane. It honked a horn so loud that I felt it in my bones and I sat back down. Horns in southern Asia are an art form. Unlike Australia, people here honk just to say hello and the more intricate the horn sound, the better. Phrases like "Please Use Your Horn", "Speed Control" and "Wait for Indication" are cheerfully daubed onto the backs of large vehicles somewhere alongside the Om symbol and pictures of smug looking Buddhist and Hindu deities.

Chickens sorted, the man pulled out his phone. "Can I photograph your wife?" he asked, just as the truck entered a crossroads.

"Shouldn't you ask her?" I asked, but this question was a mistake.

He took that as permission and raised up his phone to snap a photo of her. That was bad enough, but I was pretty sure I was in the shot too and suddenly I wasn't so sure that this was an innocent chicken farmer.

What can I tell you? Paranoia is a hell of a drug. I thought about breaking his phone, about pushing him off the truck, and of worse things too, I admit. But I couldn't do that, not for a simple photo. *Calm down, mate*, I told myself. *Not everyone in the world wants to kill you.* It was maybe the biggest mistake of my life and I'll never forgive myself.

8

I've just read over what I've written so far and I realize the elephant in the room. I sound crazy paranoid. At the time I did feel like I was overreacting a bit. Not just with the guy on the truck, but the whole clandestine journey out of Melbourne. Had there even been someone at my house? Had I imagined the guy trying to stab me? My own sanity began to blur around the edges as I played and replayed those images. Like an old VHS tape, they began to get blurry once I had viewed them too much. But I had to cling to that truth. Ultimately the truth is, I think I had always had this spy game in the back of my head. Like a version of the zombie survival plan. Even so, I thought maybe I was being too paranoid, but where was the harm in that? The truth is I simply wasn't paranoid enough.

From Kashmore, we called Dante. He had collected everything on my list and planned to meet us in Islamabad. I called him from a payphone (remember those?) using a phone card (or those?) and we spoke in generalities. On my walk back to the guesthouse, I felt strange, like I was being followed. A few of the people staring at me looked familiar. But this was a place where there were always a thousand people on the streets, all of them staring. There was no way to know.

I got back at the same time as Nova. She had picked up a trove of street food including nihari, biryani, samosas, and pakora. The whole feast cost less than five bucks, and we devoured it at the small table in our guesthouse room. Yes, we shared a room. It was safer and, before you ask, we each had our own bed.

Only after the last crumb of the last samosa was done and dusted did she ask. "Dante?"

I nodded. "He'll join us next stop."

"Good. So what's the plan, boss?" She had a serious tone but a bit of mint chutney just to the left of her mouth belied her seriousness.

I had been thinking about that very question so much that I had no answer for it. No answer other than the very obvious one. "Reckon it's time."

I reached into my inner vest pocket, unzipped it, and pulled out the map. Of course I had been studying it when I could, when I was sure that no one other than Nova was around. But this was the first time we would both have unlimited time to examine it.

The paper was old. Some forgers are good at making paper look old, but both Nova and I were skilled in deciding the truth of that. After half an hour, we had determined that the paper was from before the 18th century. It was what we in the business call "laid paper," made on a mesh made of strong wires. It had small, reddish-brown spots across the paper called foxing. The edges were brittle and the ink had faded into the paper. There was a small impression made from a letterpress on the writing. It was, in short, as old as it appeared.

I had taken all that in before I bought it, but now I could confirm it. There was an illustration so faded we had to look very carefully. It looked like an eagle with its beak in the stomach of a supine man.

"Is that who I think it is?" she asked.

I nodded. It had to be and that meant it could only be in one place. "We might have a slight detour in our itinerary."

***

We left our guesthouse early the next morning. The streets were already hot and full of people, but we made our way quickly to the station, breaking the hearts of only a few would-be rickshaw drivers. The people running the 'public' bus from Kashmore to Islamabad didn't inspire great confidence. The ticket office doubled as a restaurant and store: a slightly seedy restaurant called, appropriately enough, Pakistan Restaurant and a store called, as you might have guessed, Pakistan Store that sold lifeless snakes bobbing, their pale dead eyes trained on nothing in particular. As I enquired about the bus service, this was how the conversation went.

"We need to go today," I said, not for the first time.

"I have VIP van go on Sunday," he said, pointing to an empty parking lot.

"We need to go today."

"Hello my very good friend. How are you, I'm fine? Where you from?" Was this bizarre non-sequitur meant to throw me? I stayed firm.

"We need to go. From here to Islamabad. Today," I repeated.

"Yes, yes."

"How much is it?"

He looked at the ceiling and held his chin for a while before wagging his head and saying "Cheap, cheap."

"How cheap, cheap?" I asked. He produced the ubiquitous calculator from nowhere and quoted a figure that was about 25 percent less than the public bus.

I played it cool. "Hmmm."

"Where you go after Islamabad?"

"Not sure," I said.

"Islamabad very far. Driver will take you to Lahore. Much closer."

“What about Islamabad?” I asked. Lahore wasn’t in my schedule.

He shook his head sadly. “No go to there.”

I started again. It took another half hour and an ever increasing price (meticulously typed out on the calculator again and again) but eventually we crammed onto the right bus and then only an hour after that we were away. The journey was slated to take twenty-eight hours (Dante would beat us there), but Nova and I both knew even that lengthy time would be the best case scenario. From buses breaking down to extended stops, to road construction, there were a thousand possible delays. We were prepared for the worst, we thought, only the worst was so much worse than we could have guessed.

9

The cockroaches marched past like a victorious army. The platform was entirely theirs: all they were missing was flags and ticker tape as they marched their way down the hideously filthy platform toward the body of a man who lay unconscious in a chunky pile of his own puke. In front of us a toddler joined the hordes of others who'd stopped to stare at us, his eyes as wide open as his mouth. The toddler's pants were down and as we watched, he squatted down and pooped wetly on the train platform.

"That's not the most pleasant thing I've ever seen," Nova said. She had a weird little smile on her face though. Her green eyes sparkled with disgusted amusement.

Fearing that killing the hours sitting on this grubby platform waiting for our train might result in contracting some form of serious bacterial infection, we moved to a grubby little restaurant across the road from the station which, it turned out, had rats running along the curtain rails and a waiter who held the drinks he delivered to the table so that his fingerprints remained around the lip of the glass and you got the scent of his cigarettes with every sip. A nice touch I thought.

At this stage we'd been off the bus for just over two hours. I swear to god I'm not being paranoid but I seriously freaked out. The bus had stopped alongside an empty field. The women's side had a rough tent erected on one side that gave some privacy to them but men just dropped their trousers and just did their business (that's one and two, mind you) in front of the entire world.

I had just added my own personal contribution and I turned, still zipping, when I suddenly bumped into two men. One of them, with wavy hair and a beard that had just graduated from five o'clock shadow, was texting on his phone. I glanced at the bright screen reflexively and had to hide my shock. Now my Urdu is not great (it's always tough to read right to left) but I can make my way through it given enough time. It didn't take Noam bloody Chomsky to read the first couple of words anyway.

Look, if I can be bloody honest about it, I had come to the idea that I had overreacted. All of this cloak and dagger stuff was beginning to feel a bit silly. Now my panic returned tenfold. Fighting my urge to run or scream, I stepped up onto the bus, grabbed my Macpac and Nova's Kathmandu branded one, then found her as she exited the women's tent.

Her look of barely concealed disgust from the fumes of the tent changed into concern as she saw me approach with our bags in hand.

"What?" she said.

"Just start walking." I grabbed her elbow and steered, walking at a barely sub-frantic pace. We went around the tent, so it stood between us and the line of sight of the bus and off we scurried into the field. It was a mostly brown patch of earth dotted with cabbages and wild tufts of grass. Nothing large enough to hide us, unfortunately, but we moved through it quickly enough.

"What the hell, boss?" she said after a couple of minutes.

My heart was beating so loudly in my ears that I barely heard her. Taking a deep breath, I glanced back. The bus had left without us. But were we alone? Had the two men I'd seen gotten back on the bus? There was no sign of them, but the tent blocked part of the view.

I stopped walking and turned to face her. "I bumped into a fella who was texting. In Urdu, so I don't know everything he said. But the first words were: Jad Malek and friend."

"Crikey. That's not the best news I've heard all day," she said tersely. We walked on, through fields of cabbages for an hour or so, cautiously accepting rides from a pair of pre-teens on motorbikes when we got to a road ("Do you like Pakistan?") and that's how we reached Rahim Yar Khan and bought train tickets for a train that would not come.

***

Author's Note: I'm not sure if there are missing pages or if Uncle Jad never finished writing this part, but I've combed through everything and the rest of this part of the story doesn't seem to exist. I'm not actually sure what happened but when the story picks up he's coming from a part of southern China I didn't know much about. I'd give a lot to know what happened but there are only a few tantalizing hints and I dare not speculate. I'll let you come to whatever conclusions you choose.

10

Kodari was beautiful. I don't mean the pink and orange hues of the sunrise nor the crispness of the clear, cold air that held our breaths before us or the quiet and stillness of the empty village first thing in the morning. I mean the welcoming sight and feel of the unmoving, absolutely solid earth beneath my feet. Fifty-nine somewhat trying hours after leaving, passing through Xinjiang, meeting Dante, and then departing Lanzhou on the so-called "Lhasa Express," I wanted nothing more than to feel stationary, to walk without bracing myself against walls and doors, to listen and not hear the rhythmic clatter of rails and to look at a fixed point on the landscape without it sliding by. If there's time I might write later about Xinjiang. There truly are too many interesting things to write about in Xinjiang, including the Tocharian culture, the red haired mummies in the museum of Urumqi, and the camel statues, but none of that is pertinent to this story.

The Chinese border post beside the Tibetan hillside town of Zhangmu is a state-of-the-art, modern piece of grand Chinese architecture boasting x-ray machines, smartly uniformed guards and a fully integrated computerised passport scanning and identification system. The Nepalese border post, on the other hand, is a rickety barn with bars on the windows, a squat toilet visible from the immigration queue that even the flies are disgusted by, and a staff consisting of local guys in hoodies with ink and cigarette stained fingers who peer curiously at you, the frustrated tourist, from behind tinted glasses.

If it was heavenly to be on *terra firma*, it was equally otherworldly to be back in Nepal. Despite poor transport infrastructure and despite a turbulent political situation and despite third world health care conditions, everything had that colorful, relaxed feel about it and is largely played out in front of a backdrop of snow-capped mountains so magnificent and pointy under the azure blue sky that it could have been painted by Miyazaki. There's a sense that nothing bad can really happen and if it does, they'll just paint over it with bright colors.

We sat in a small cafe on the edge of the only road in town while we waited for the next jeep. The cafe was staffed by a young woman with broad shoulders and long dark hair. It had been a rough night. Though we were at the relatively low elevation of 2,300 meters, we had been up as high as 5,300 meters over the last couple of days. Anything above 2,700 meters can result in Acute Mountain Sickness (AMS) and it had taken its toll on all of us. Nova most of all. Her face had a green tinge and I had heard her puking last night. Nausea was one of the symptoms of AMS. If only she could have been painted over with bright colors and improved too! Instead she ordered a glass of mint tea. I ordered ginger tea in a big thermos.

"How you going?" I asked her.

The look she gave me was almost unreadable.

"I'm whelmed, boss," she said. That was one of our little jokes. She was not overwhelmed. She wasn't underwhelmed. She was simply whelmed.

"And Dante? You charming unpleasant person you. How you going? You're not tired from carrying those bags?"

He looked at me, not sure why I was going through this particular charade.

"It's easy for me," he said. Behind him were two enormous tucker bags. They were old leather stuffed full with supplies, equipment, and even some actual tucker for when we got hungry. I could not have carried both of them, not if I wanted to keep my vertebrae intact, but Dante was as strong as he was silent.

"I'm going to tell you some interesting facts about Nepal," I told him. "One, Nepal has the only triangular flag in the world. Everyone else defaults to rectangle. But here, they respect the mountains. Two, the world's only living goddess resides here. You'll probably see her in Kathmandu. Three, seventy-five percent of all women here have never touched a drop of alcohol. I'm sure Nova will drop that percentage a few points."

She cheersed me with an imaginary martini glass. But Dante only looked thoughtful and said, "Interesting."

There was a long silence and then Nova said, "For a moment, nothing happened. Then, after a second or so, nothing continued to happen."

We all laughed at the reference. Even Dante, who wasn't much of a reader, was a fan of Douglas Adams. He listened to them on audiobook which, in my opinion, isn't really reading, but I appreciated the effort.

The dark-haired young woman brought our teas and disappeared out the back. Dante munched on some chewy *balep korkun* (Tibetan flat bread) while Nova mournfully stirred her mint tea. I looked at her bleary face and felt a stab of sympathy. "You want this ginger tea too?" I asked. Ginger helped settle the stomach and deal with high altitudes. It was no cocoa leaf in terms of effectiveness, but it tasted much better. I had ordered it more out of boredom than any real thirst.

She considered for half-a-second. "Yeah alright." I slid the thermos over to her and thought about the upcoming day. We had a lot of ground to cover and in this part of the world it could take twelve hours to go 100 kilometers. At least we had lost our pursuers. I remember thinking this exact thought: *The mad journey out of Pakistan had succeeded.* What a dickhead.

Nova choked and spluttered. There was no traffic going by on the main road, it was still early, but from somewhere I heard the sound of a motorcycle starting up and accelerating away at a desperate pace. *That bloke is in an unpleasant person-ing hurry*, I thought.

Dante and I smiled, not understanding. "Strong tea?" I asked her.

Nova's face turned red. The cup fell from her hand and clattered on the cold wooden floor. Her elbow knocked the big thermos down as she clumsily scrambled to her feet. Her cold fingers reached for her throat.

Even then it hadn't sunk in. "You know you can't choke on tea," I said, or something very like it. But I glanced at Dante. The smile had fallen from his face and he had risen to his feet. His expression was a thundercloud. I looked back at Nova.

It all happened so fast. Her face was going black and she made a terrible sound as she clawed at her throat with all her strength, as if trying to remove two invisible, implacable hands. The light in her green eyes was dimming rapidly.

"Jesus Christ," I sprang to my feet, sending my chair crashing to the floor. I glanced around but the woman who had been serving us was gone. "Call an ambulance," I shouted to no one in particular. This was a useless thing to say for more than one reason. There was no one to make that call, and no ambulances for hundreds of kilometers.

Nova collapsed on the ground, her body limply wriggling. I jumped over to her and jammed my fingers in her throat.

Strong hands pulled me off. "Don't induce vomiting," Dante said. "Doesn't work."

Her body had gone still. I grabbed her wrist and it felt like the world had ended. No pulse. There was no pulse.

It was hard to see suddenly. I wiped at my eyes as the sense of being helpless, useless, and worthless overwhelmed me. All my strength and resolve evacuated my body all at once.

Dante reached into his jacket and pulled out a long gleaming knife.

"What are you doing?"

His eyes narrowed but did not meet mine. "Poison," he said. "Stay here." So saying, he sprang away toward the back of the kitchen.

I sat down on the cold floor next to Nova's cold body. Her green eyes were open and staring in shock up at the ceiling. It felt like I sat there for a long time, alone, alone, alone.

"The hero fold," I said in a small voice, to no one whatsoever.

11

Dante and I ended up staying in bloody Kodari for three more days. It took half a day for Dante to get back from his (unsuccessful) pursuit. And then we had to talk first to Lieutenant Thapa of the Nepalese Army and then the police and then to Lieutenant Thapa again. It had just about ended when they discovered the lifeless body of the woman who owned the little cafe we had drank in. She was lying face down in her home. We saw photos and it definitely was not the woman who served us, though neither the police nor Lieutenant Thapa could (or would) tell us anything more.

I tried to remember the person who served us but I honestly hadn't paid attention. She had left on a motorcycle immediately after serving the tea. Dante had borrowed a bike of his own, at knife point, which is another reason the police talked to us for so long. Whoever it was, they had gotten away and Dante couldn't find them.

At last we sat in a small guesthouse room. I rested on one of the dingy single beds while he paced and stared out the window. The room wasn't much but at 100 rupees, it was a bit of a bargain really, even though I could see the outside world through the slats.

"I want you to fly back with her," I said. Getting her body back to Australia was a whole mess but we had worked it out. He didn't actually have to accompany the body but it made sense.

His expression was black and bleak and broken. "Her sister is on the way. I'll come with you." His voice was toneless.

"We're in the middle of nowhere, mate. Pain in the arse for Georgia to get out here. Come on. You know it's the right call."

"I know that when you take on that tone, you're trying to sell me something," he said. "Wheedle all you want. I'm not buying."

"Look, don't be an unpleasant person about it," I said. "She needs you more than I do."

"She's dead," he said. "She doesn't need anything."

"You know what I mean," I said.

"No, I don't. Why are you trying to get rid of me?"

"It's dangerous to be around me."

"No kidding. We knew that. Both of us. Tell me what's really going on."

"Why are you talking so much?" I asked. "I prefer the quiet you."

He was standing in front of me now. I could see the dust caking his boots and legs.

I looked at the flower pattern on the blanket and avoided his eyes. In my mind's eye, I saw *her* clawing at her throat again. Why the fuck hadn't I known what was going on? If I had realized it earlier, maybe I could have saved her.

"Look at me," Dante growled. I slowly looked up at the volcano of a man. Rage simmered deep in his core and I knew part of it was aimed at me. I knew that I deserved it too.

"She knew the risks. You didn't kill her."

Fuck. He could have sucker punched me in the gut and it wouldn't have hit as hard.

Tears again filled my eyes and when I spoke it was in a strange voice.

"I didn't even need the tea," I said. "I as good as poisoned her myself."

"Flip that. You think the assassin would have just gone home? Probably all three of us would have died."

The damn dam broke. I jumped to my feet and pushed him away. I pushed hard but it only made him take half a step back. "Look mate. I shouldn't have bought the bloody map. I shouldn't have had you two join when I did. I shouldn't have gotten the bloody tea." All of the fury left my body with those words and I collapsed onto the bed. "Mate, I'm so sorry. I fucked up."

He sat down beside me and put his arm around me. "You're a galah. But you're my kind of galah. I'm staying with you."

A knot of tension I was not aware of broke within me. The truth is, it had been an honest offer. But I had this feeling in the back of my head that without Dante, I wasn't going to last.

"Hey," Dante said. "It's okay to have a whinge. Remember when Nova spewed in my eye?"

I laughed and it hurt my stomach. "She just chugged that Pepsi and leaned over, getting ready to let out the largest belch ever," I continued.

"So she looks up at me," Dante said. We had told this story many times, usually in front of her to embarrass her. "And I know what's coming. I try to pre-empt her, so I concentrate on getting a big burp ready. She saw that and hurried to release a terrible burp reeking of Pepsi fumes. But instead of a belch, she threw up bile and Pepsi in my eye."

I could barely talk. I was laughing so hard. "Mate, you ran to the toilet screaming 'You barfed in my eye.'"

We both laughed there, sitting on the bed. And then we both cried. And then, some time after that, we were ready for business again.

"I really could use a bloody drink, mate," Dante said.

12

Kathmandu is just over a hundred kilometers from Kodari. Back home, on the Hume Freeway, that would be an hour's drive. It took us *significantly* longer.

We were out of the door by 4:10 in the morning and the jeep arrived shortly after. This was best case scenario, close to the time it was actually scheduled, but in true Nepali fashion it was merely to drive backwards, half-an-hour to another town, over a dark bumpy road. Three guys got in and all sat in the middle row, with me, shoulder to shoulder. The back was empty, Dante sat in the front, and there we were, four men needlessly pressed together. All of our bags, including his two massive ones, were strapped to the top of the jeep.

By five in the morning we moved on and gained/lost people. Now there were three people in every layer, save for the middle where we now had five somehow. At a quarter to seven, we stopped for a tea break. It was light and the roads were swarming with people walking on their daily business. As a night owl, it's always nice for me to be up early in the morning. Still it had been almost three hours on the road and we had gone, what, maybe twelve kilometers total. We climbed back into the jeep and listened to hours and hours of very loud filmi music.

At 8:30 we changed jeeps. The only bit of excitement before that was the guy behind me spewing all over the place. It took some time to get going, but we all got back into the same places and eventually rumbled back down the mountain.

Progress was very stop-and-go. Even when it was a go, it was slow, over new roads and through dusty river valleys. But mostly we stopped as serious construction was taking place. Lots of new bridges were nearly built and the road was paved in many areas. We avoided all those and snailed along as quickly as we could.

We stopped for a good dal bhat with a great potato curry around noon. I was hoping that we were within six hours of Kathmandu but without phones it was hard to tell. We left and drove through a long river valley. It's beautiful in an entirely different way than the mountains we had been traveling through: hundreds of people, goats, water buffalo, children playing and swimming, and just so much life everywhere.

But there was so much construction too. After lunch, we stopped a minimum of ten times to see a dump truck slowly loaded with rocks and dirt from caterpillars. Each break took between fifteen and thirty minutes as buses, cars, and motorcycles impatiently queued on the narrow roads.

A few times we found tarmac and sped up to heady heights of twenty or thirty kilometers an hour. It would always devolve into crazy winding paths through villages or up mountains, though.

At 5:30 pm we stopped for tea and I got some fly-covered, cold, and quite old aloo and roti for 50 cents. I spoke a few words to Dante and we began to worry that we'd get to Kathmandu late enough that finding a room could be a problem. I spoke with a bloke in my simple Hindi who told me we were 2.5-3 hours away from Kathmandu now.

At 6:30 we stopped for gas at the "Buddha Oil." One of the four blokes in the middle got out and though he was temporarily replaced by a man with a chicken, we ended up only having three guys in the middle from here on out. Much better, though the music was still at full blast.

It started to look like we were in Kathmandu around 7:30. There were more houses and people and businesses. Some people got out but we stayed in, waiting to see something familiar. Eventually at 9 pm we were at the end of the line. Kathmandu is the kind of city that pretty much shuts down as the sun sets so Dante and I discussed options. We wanted to get to Thamel, the touristic center of the city, and realized we would have to catch a cab. The bus exchange had plenty of cab drivers here.

You kind of know that the first couple of cabbies that come up to you are going to be a bit shit. We tried to walk past them all, but a persistent guy kept following us. "Come with me. Taxi. 500 rupees." The price should be 250, so we ignored him.

"Come on, how much you want?" he asked.

"300 hundred," we said, thinking this low price would drive him away.

There was no hesitation. "Okay, 300 okay. Let's go." This should have been a warning sign. We walked with him across the parking lot, to his old car and he said, "I am not taxi driver. I am hotel driver. You stay at my hotel and taxi is free."

We could have still said no and found a different taxi to take us to Thamel. But sometimes it's easier just to go with the flow. As we talked, we were surrounded by ten or twelve people who seemed not so much curious about the conversation or us but just really interested in seeing how well they could surround us.

"How much is the room?"

"Very nice room. You will like it."

"I do like very nice rooms. How much is it?"

Dante and I were both well aware of the twinkle in his eyes as his brain conducted some advanced algebra to figure out a price that would be lower than we would pay but not so high that we didn't just leave.

"Ten dollars," he said. "Very good room. Double room, big bed, attached bathroom, just stay one night and go somewhere else tomorrow. Good room."

This was very cheap and, hey, free cab ride. Another man showed up and they promised to drop us off at the hotel free of charge. We agreed and climbed in.

I mentioned he had an old car, and it fully struggled with the two of us in the back seat, three big backpacks in the boot, and two Nepali unpleasant people in the front. The car kept stopping and one of them would get out and kick the tire or something and we'd rumble forward again. The road did us no favors. It was unsealed, had more potholes than road, and weaved up and down. At last, the brave car came to a stop and couldn't be revived.

They didn't say anything to us, but one of the guys took off down the road. Five minutes later he was back in a smaller car that was equally old but still driving. This car had less room and we threw two of our big bags on the roof. No ropes or anything to tie them down, just rested them there. Like particularly underwhelming clowns, we clambered back into the car.

It had begun to feel like the day that would never end, but at last we got to our hotel. We were shown a nice room, and nodding appreciatively, we asked, "Ten dollars?"

The guy laughed as though this was a scandalous suggestion. "No, no. This is not ten dollar room."

"Then show us the ten dollar room, please," I said.

He led us to a dorm room, with no attached bathroom, and switched on the light. A few beleaguered denizens of the dorm blinked at us in surprise. Dante and I looked at each other, more amused than anything else. Of course they were taking the piss. We argued with him a bit, and the upshot was we agreed on the original room for twelve bucks (including tax).

There were two beds and thick blankets and after we locked the doors, the windows, and checked the room just in case, we fell asleep immediately. I knew the assassin was still out there but the day's travels had exhausted me in a profound way and I slept. I dreamt of the moon, glowing brighter than the sun.

13

It was hard to take a picture of Kathmandu because there's always so much going on. Taking a picture of one aspect leaves another four out. Kathmandu isn't a photogenic city in that there exist iconic photos, but it's a fantastic one in terms of the vibe.

The first thing I did was to buy some patchwork clothes and hiking boots. This was traveler camouflage of the best kind, and if you think a guy my age can't blend in with the traveling crowd, well you'd be right in a lot of countries but Nepal plays by its own rules. Second, I picked up an old iPhone, with no sim card that I used to take photos. It helped me to blend in. Dante wore a different kind of disguise: blue jeans and black t-shirt. Other than his powerful physique, he looked like any guy in any place anywhere.

We got food and ate in our room. (We were both too much on edge to dare eating out.) We silently finished our chips and falafel, which were surprisingly good, and then he looked at me.

"We got a problem," he said.

We, in fact, had several problems but I knew what he meant. "This map," I began, but he shook his head.

"It's not the map, per se. It's the killers that come with it."

"Yeah no," I said. "That's true. Why are they after us?"

"The why is easy. The map is invaluable. A treasure worth killing for. The question we have to answer is: who? Trained assassins aren't so common in real life. And most of them work for the government or private security forces."

"Reckon it could be either of those," I said.

He frowned. "Could be," he said in a tone that meant the opposite. "But this is some kind of private organization. They want the map either for the profit or …" he trailed off.

"Or to protect themselves," I finished. "This map leads to some secret conspiracy who has access to information they shouldn't and killers who show no compunction."

"What could it be?" he asked. "What could be so valuable? No, we can't guess. Let's just agree it's something valuable to someone. But consider the facts. You were attacked initially within minutes of getting the map. Your home was tossed. You did the right thing. Left the country right away, with a fake ID. Travelled overland through countries without surveillance. And yet you were tracked. You were made on a dirt road in rural Pakistan. That shit can't happen by accident. Then you zigged. We met up in China. They can't have tracked that. But they immediately found us over the border. What does all that mean?"

Of course I had lived it, but hearing Dante describe it all so matter-of-factly gave me the chills. "They may as well be the unpleasant person-ing Illuminati, they are that all-knowing."

"Right," he said. "We have to assume they can find us anywhere. That they have eyes on us at all times. They can get an assassin in our midst anywhere in the world. That leaves us with two possible responses, both of which I recommend we need to undertake as soon as possible. We need reinforcements. Professionals. How much money have you got?"

"Enough," I said. "I can get my hands on more if need be." Money was not a problem for me. I had earned well throughout my lifetime and had a few million hidden here and there.

He looked at me seriously. "Need be. And that's point two. If they can track us anywhere, we need to take it to them. We can't fend them off indefinitely. So far they have attempted to be precise. I assume because they want the map back. They may change their mind. A building or car we are in could blow up. We can't assume they won't be successful next time."

I resisted the urge to point out they had already been successful. He knew it better than I. "It makes sense," I said. "But … how? Where are they? We don't even know who they are."

He shrugged. "*Who* doesn't matter. *Where* matters. Of course they could be anywhere."

There was a noise in the hallway and he stopped talking. Without saying anything we both moved off the beds and ducked low. I held my breath, thinking bullets might come flying through the door at any second but the noise died down. It was just someone going to their room.

Dante moved to the door and listened before returning to his spot on his bed. "We don't know where they are. We can't afford to search the world and hope to get lucky. So we make a big assumption."

"A gamble, huh? Is it time to hold or time to fold?"

"It's always time to hold. Only losers fold," Dante said. The qualities that made him a good man made him a poor gambler. "Let's see that map."

He looked at it carefully before sighing in exaggerated relief. "Phew," he said. "It's definitely not Kazakhstan. I was sure we would end up there again."

"No," I said. "It's a different part of the former USSR. Have a look at this." I pointed at the illustration of the man and the bird.

He waited for me to say more. “I don’t know where that is,” he said. “I am not the deep lore expert that you are….” He trailed off and we both knew he had almost added, “and that Nova is.”

“The myth of Prometheus comes from the ancient land of Colchis.” He frowned in concentration upon hearing that name. “Sound familiar? Colchis is where Jason and the Argonauts supposedly found the Golden Fleece. It was a land full of wealth and sorcery.”

“Okay, Professor.”

This was his polite way of reminding me to get to the point, and I have to admit that he wasn’t wrong. “The man, or technically Titan, getting his liver eaten by a raven is none other than Prometheus. And the Prometheus Cave is found in modern day Georgia. Once known as Colchis.”

“That’s one of the few countries I haven’t been to yet,” he said evenly. For Dante, this was the equivalent of jumping up and down on his bed screaming with joy.

“The caves are in the western part of the country, near Kutaisi. It will take longer but we should travel overland. We’ll head back through India, across southern Pakistan and Iran and then come up through Armenia or Azerbaijan. What?”

He was staring at me as if I had grown a second head. “Mate, that’s 15,000 kilometers away. We don’t have time.”

“We’re not flying,” I said. “Too easy to track.”

“Ten hours or two months,” he said. “Easy choice.”

“We’re not flying.”

He walked over to the window and peered cautiously through the curtains. A troop of monkeys clambered across the rooftops.

“Dante, listen to me. We’re not flying.”

He didn’t even bother to rebut me. The decision had been made.

14

Three days later we stood pressed together at Tribhuvan International Airport. This is, I have been told repeatedly, one of the only airports in the world where you can see monkeys, although thankfully there were none today. At least not yet. As always there were dozens or hundreds of people flying with massive boxes taped closed. What was unusual was that three of them, as of yesterday, worked for me. And though they dressed as simple Newari laborers, they were actually former Gurkhas and the sight of them calmed me.

***

Hi, it's me, the nephew, again. Sorry to interrupt, but if you, like me, don't know who or what a Gurkha is then I'm here to explain. Gurkhas are high altitude soldiers with a reputation as some of the world's most skilled and fearsome warriors. To become a Gurka, one must undergo an incredibly demanding selection process. Every year, 20,000 incredibly fit people try out and only two or three hundred are chosen. They must do seventy-five bench jumps in one minute, then seventy sit-ups in two minutes. That's just the warm up! They then run five kilometers up a mountain, carrying 25 kg of rocks on their back, and they have to finish in under an hour.

Their history is incredible. A small force of them fought the British Empire to a standstill in the 19th century. The British were so impressed that they drafted them into their army, where they still serve. They fought in both World Wars winning 2,000 awards for gallantry in the First World War alone. Their motto is "Better to die than be a coward," and they are skilled in hand-to-hand combat, particularly with their traditional weapon, the kukri. (Kukris are long, curved knives.) I could go on and on but you get the idea. These guys were legit.

***

Despite everything, I was feeling good. I realized I had been stuck in Melbourne for too long. Don't get me wrong, Melbourne is a fantastic city (certainly much better than Sydney) but I hadn't left it for more than a week or two for a couple of years. I needed to travel again, to get jarred out of the insulation and protection of routines. I was raw again, new in ways that felt both simultaneously painful and terrific.

Dante was dressed in a full tuxedo. He had reasoned (and I couldn't argue with him) that if we were doomed to be watched and followed, he wanted it to be done in style. He also had, hidden deep in a pocket we had stealthily sewn ourselves, the map. I was not well pleased with that, but once he had pointed out that I was the obvious target, it made sense. So I stayed in the "disguise" of my traveler clothes, with a colorful stocking cap and some prayer flags draped across my Macpac. His disguise was obvious, no disguise at all. The old hiding in plain sight trick. It wasn't a bad plan, even in retrospect. But there was something we hadn't counted on.

I was ready for a knife-wielding assailant, a sniper taking a shot, or poison in my tea. I hadn't considered an obstacle of the more official nature. As I handed my passport to the customs agent, I didn't think twice. It was a fake passport, but it was a very expensive fake passport. I had flown in and out of the UK and the US and EU with it. But the man's stern look grew sterner. He called over another agent and they said something. It was not in Nepali (Nepal has over 100 languages) and I didn't follow, but I had a sinking feeling in my stomach.

Dante, on the other hand, was already through. Well that was a relief. He paused for a moment, glancing back at me. I nodded with my eyes, indicating he should keep going. His insistence on carrying the map now felt inspired.

"Can you come with us, my good sir?" the immigration companion said to me as two guards with machine guns came up behind him.

"What seems to be the problem?" I asked.

"Come with us. We will explain."

I hate to play the ugly tourist but I had to try. "Excuse me," I said in a loud voice. "I am an AMERICAN citizen. And I need to catch my plane. What right do you have to speak to me this way? I want to talk to a lawyer."

My American accent isn't great. It wouldn't pass muster in New York or Chicago, but I got my a's to sound nasally enough. This passport was American, with one of my favorite aliases: Randy Lincoln. Randy. That word, which means something very different to non-Yanks, almost made me laugh out loud right there. The line of people behind me grew as there were only a few customs officers working at this point.

The immigration boss looked at the man who had stopped me with uncertainty. I felt a moment of hope that this bluff could succeed. Unfortunately, the agent knew what he was about.

"Fake," he said, looking right at me.

Look, getting caught with a fake passport at an airport is fucked. I was facing a few possible consequences, including immediate detainment (and Nepalese jail is no picnic, I can assure you that), seizure and investigation of my goods, criminal charges for forgery and fraud, heavy fines, and a possible travel ban.

I have no idea what I would have done if those monkeys hadn't appeared throwing pieces of dried mud and poo at everyone in the line. Some people screamed or cursed but most people pulled out their phones to record it.

"Hey, stop that," the officer said. "You can't record here."

A man bumped me and I turned, thinking I was being attacked. It was Mr Thapa, one of my bodyguards, but he was here acting a bit subterfuge.

"Move," he said imperiously. "I have to catch my flight too."

The man who had stopped me had risen. He opened his mouth to say something and that was when he was hit in the forehead with a piece of something brown and not entirely dry.

He cursed and ducked down. I grabbed my passport and moved past him, walking as slowly as I dared. I met Dante only a minute away in the duty free shop. The smell of perfume wafted over to me as I pointed behind me and mouthed "The monkeys?" He looked confused and shook his head.

I walked up to him and had a look at the whisky, noting that Talisker was a good price. "I can't explain what happened. Someone was tipped off. I got lucky, I guess. But we have got an hour before our flight. As soon as all that monkey business dies down, they'll be after me."

He shook his head. "The low level guy was after you but his boss wasn't. If they do come after you for a fake passport, tell them you're seeking asylum, or swear you didn't know your passport was wrong. Tell them it must have happened at the hotel. That can mitigate consequences. Offer to pay a convenience fee. Tell them you won't come back. They won't make trouble."

I stared at him. "How do you know so much about this?" He shrugged.

"Subterfuge. It's easy for me," he said. I hated when he said that, but just this once I didn't mind. And in the end, we got on the flight. I had no idea what had happened but it was clear that things were escalating. I was glad we were flying instead of going overland. *Soon this will all be over.* I actually thought that, dickhead that I am.

And look, before we move on, I know, I know. Getting saved by monkeys is a weird situation to be in. If I was telling a story, I would have made up something better. Something where I did something fully awesome and escaped by leaping on the plane at the last second. But I have to tell it like it happened. And that happened. You can check YouTube and see footage of it if you don't believe me.

15

We sat next to each other on the plane. The echo of my flight with Nova rang loudly and amidst my sorrow suddenly I worried about Dante. Not so much about him, but what I would do without him. I realized of course that I was panicking, but that didn't stop me from sliding further down into panic mode. So I did what I always do. I used my words.

"So, as I was saying, Colchis had the Golden Fleece. Jason arrived to take it, to prove to old King Pelias that he was worthy of the throne. Of course, the old king had stolen the throne and sent Jason to the far ends of the earth on what was meant to be a wild goose chase."

"I know," Dante said. "I've seen the Harryhausen flick. Dope skeletons."

"Yeah, yeah, everyone knows the story," I agreed, not stopping. "But the thing is, they know the Greek side of things. The Colchiseans were fairly put upon."

"Unfairly put on," he said, in a rare attempt at humor.

"Exactly. I mean there they were, minding their own bloody business when this guy Jason gathers up all kinds of heroes, including bloody Hercules, shows up, steals the treasure, steals the king's daughter, murders the king's son, and then goes home as a hero. It's fucked when you think about it."

The flight attendant came by and offered us snacks and drinks. We declined both. That had been a hard lesson learned and neither of us were likely to eat food from a stranger for a long time. I looked behind me and saw a mostly full flight, even though we would get into Tbilisi at three in the morning. For some reason, most flights to Georgia seemed to arrive in the middle of the night.

"But let me ask you this," I said, ignoring that a few minutes had gone by since I had last spoken. "What did the Golden Fleece do? Why was it so valuable?"

"Made out of gold, I reckon."

"Sure, but there was gold closer by and in larger quantities. Better treasures too. No, that's the part the Greeks got wrong. The Golden Fleece wasn't a treasure. It was a source of knowledge."

"Say more."

"Well in Georgia, they tell you it was a book of medicine. Like a Web MD or Gray's Anatomy of its time. The keeper of it was the king's daughter, in this case Medea. It's no coincidence that both the book and the woman were taken."

"You're talking like it was real."

"The story is real," I said. "I'm not a historian. History is worthless anyway. What I care about is the story attached to something."

"Are you telling me," Dante said. His tone was incredulous. "Are you trying to say that you expect to find the golden fleece at the end of this map?"

I laughed. "Well, the thought had occurred, but no. That would be bizarre. But Medea as the source of medicine is interesting. What did Jason need to cure? And remember, while Medea ended up with a bad rep, that was at the hands of noted woman hater Euripides. Jason and the Argonauts had at least ten plays in Ancient Greece. They were the original cinematic universe. They must have done something important. Remember, most heroes belonged to a city. You had Theseus in Athens or Hercules in Thebes. But Jason was renowned throughout northern Greece. He transcended the city state."

"Interesting," Dante said.

"Yes it is," I agreed, even though I suspected he wasn't earnest in his appraisal.

"But it's not the fleece that brings us there. It's Prometheus," Dante pointed out.

"Exactly. Is it related to the fleece? It's hard to say. Unlikely. But we can't rule it out."

"Tell me again about Prometheus. Keep it short."

"Class, today we're diving into one of the most fascinating myths of Greek mythology: the tale of Prometheus. We're dealing with themes like creation, rebellion, punishment, and the pursuit of knowledge."

"Fast forward," he said.

"Prometheus, whose name means 'forethought,' was a Titan. Remember, the Titans were an older generation of gods who held power before Zeus and the Olympians came to power. Prometheus, however, was unique. Unlike many Titans who opposed Zeus, Prometheus aligned himself with the Olympians during their war against the Titans. For his loyalty, Zeus allowed him to live up on Mt. Olympus after the war."

"Get to the part that matters."

"But Prometheus had a rebellious streak. He cared deeply for humanity, a creation of the gods. In some versions of the myth, Prometheus is even credited with shaping humans out of clay. However, the early humans were weak, ignorant, and lacked the tools to survive. Zeus, the king of the gods, decreed that humanity should remain in this primitive state. Why, you ask? Because Zeus wanted to maintain the clear divide between mortals and gods, and he feared humanity becoming too powerful."

"Okay, that part I can understand," Dante said. "Some things never change."

"Prometheus defied this order. In his most famous act, he stole fire from Mount Olympus and gifted it to humanity. Now, let's pause here. Fire in this context isn't just literal flame (though it was certainly that) but also a symbol of knowledge, technology, and civilization. With fire, humans could cook, forge tools, create art, and establish a foundation for progress. And they could heal."

"Link to the Fleece?" he asked.

"I imagine so. Zeus, of course, was enraged. He saw Prometheus's actions as an unforgivable betrayal. To punish him, Zeus devised a gruesome and eternal torment. Prometheus was chained to a rock in the Caucasus Mountains where every day, a raven would swoop down and devour his liver. Being immortal, Prometheus's liver would regenerate each night, only for the cycle to repeat the next day. Eventually, Hercules, who sailed with the Argonauts, liberated Prometheus as part of his legendary labors, shooting the raven and breaking the chains."

"Okay, okay," Dante said in a thoughtful tone.

"So the story of Prometheus is that of a symbol of the human drive to question, to create, and to progress, no matter the consequences. What does that mean about what we will find there? Your guess is as good as mine."

"Fire?" he said. "A bird. Hercules. A sheepskin. None of it makes sense."

"I know," I said. "And yet we know that there is something there, or that some people are utterly convinced there is."

"We do know that," Dante said, and with that we both fell into silence for the rest of the flight.

16

We didn't check into our hotel until 10 in the morning. The window from our room (we indeed continued to share a room for safety, and perhaps for the company as well) revealed a smattering of fading, blocky Soviet era apartments. It reminded me of the old joke: *Oh you like brutalist architecture, do you? Give me five concrete examples.* Mr Thapa and his two associates had rooms on either side of us. We were as safe as we could manage.

Though it was morning, neither of us had slept for over twenty-four hours and we both lay down to take a quick cat nap. Whether it was the psychic residue of my struggles, the night with no sleep, or just trying to sleep in the morning, I had an incredibly vivid dream the likes of which I have never had before.

I was out in space, watching the Earth like you watch television, except I could see any part I wanted. I could change my attention and see different scenes. A university professor taught a class with a delegation unexpectedly headed his way. A young woman was chased by robbers in a Hong Kong harbor. A man and a woman explored a dark mine in Africa.

I could even sense myself down there, nestled in a blanket in a room in a building in a city that, from this vantage point, sat on the very edge of an ancient range of jagged mountains. But I was only tertiarily aware of myself. Increasingly my attention was drawn across the ages. I saw a ship of bronzed men sailing through cold seas. A young woman taken from her bed at night, a sheepskin wrapped around her head to prevent her from screaming. A shirtless man cut down in the halls and a flight to the sea.

In my dream I grew warmer. There were stars all around me and they heated me like embers from a fire. One of them looked familiar and I thought, utilizing the logic of dreams, oh, I must have gone to school with that one.

I looked back down at the Earth and saw a claw of panthers (yes, that's the right word, I checked) slipping through a forest. They were hunting a fox and bear who sat at a campfire cooking a pot of food. The two animals knew the panthers were out there, that I could tell, but they didn't look up. They just ate and talked with their heads down as the panthers drew ever nearer.

"They'll be okay," the friendly looking star said to me, in star language. It was only then that I realized I was a star too. I could feel the cold vacuum of space pressing in on me on all sides. The cold of space became the cold of the sea. I swam down, deeper and deeper. There was something I needed to do but I felt unprepared. Did I have a test today? Shit. I had not studied at all.

Then I realized, and how hadn't I known it before, that I was in a submarine. But it was going down at a rapid rate and no one was at the controls. I looked around but there was no one else there on the subway. We just drove along a dark unnamed street.

And then I knew. Something was watching me. A sense of powerful malice, as if I were naked and alone on the Serengeti surrounded by unseen but not un-sensed lions, washed over me. A golden face phased in and out of the darkness. The hairs on the back of my neck rose and I awoke. "Somebody's watching me!" I blurted out to Dante, who sat in lotus position on his bed doing stretches.

My mouth was open and fresh drool slid down the right side of it. My hand reached out toward Dante with beseeching urgency, though I could barely see as the fog of recent sleep obscured my vision.

"Morning. You look a right bludger," he said calmly.

17

It occurs to me that Tbilisi in this account, just like on that trip, has gotten short shrift. Let me just take a second to tell you about it. It is an amazing city. The downtown is perched in a gorge and has an ancient fortress abutting a flowing river besides ruins and Turkish baths. Other than nearby Yerevan, also built around a gorge, there's really nowhere like it. The food is so good, including lobiani (bean stuffed bread), khachapuri (cheese filled bread) and khinkali (a dumpling with a twist: literally!). The wine is legendary and I saw with amusement that Imagine Dragons and Die Antwoord were coming to play soon.

We would spend almost zero time in this fine city, however. I still had some contacts with a few "good boys" (the term for locals who didn't always make money in legal ways, if you get my drift) from my last trip and Dante and now I sat in the back of a black Benz. Mr Thupa and one of his associates rode motorbikes in front of us and behind us, respectively. The third of their number, Mr Rai, would remain in Tbilisi and coordinate from there.

We had our big bags beside us, not in the trunk. It was uncomfortable, slightly, but at this point we were in the "be as prepared as possible" mode. Dante's large tucker bags spilled from his door to halfway across my lap, and many of the items within were hard and unyielding.

The man beside the driver was called Shurgu. He was lean and bald but had a thick mustache and beard. His arms were covered in full sleeves and he wore a short sleeve button up to go with his rectangular sunglasses and black messenger bag and the driver was an old friend of mine named Lasha. I had met him years ago and I knew he was a good bloke, if a bit full on. He had dressed down, even leaving his cane behind, for this mission. As we slowly made our honking way through traffic, Shurgu turned back to face us. He was in a good mood, one that had clearly been enhanced with a bit of the Georgia grape.

"Are you Christian?" he asked. This was a weirdly common question in these parts, the local equivalent of "Do you like Pakistan?"

I answered him without answering, and we made small talk for some time. I led him to believe that we shared sentiments on films, issues big and small, and religion too. As we finally eased out of Tbilisi, I asked the important question.

"So tell me more about this cave," I said. We had a five hour drive, and that was if things went right. Georgia was not Nepal or Pakistan, but there was always the chance of the unexpected.

Shurgu took a sip from his coffee and turned around to face me. I stared at the geometric shapes tattooed on his beefy arms.

"Krubera is the deepest cave on Earth. The Crow Cave. It goes down over 2,000 meters, is twenty kilometers long, but unlike other deep caves around the world, this wasn't explored until the 2000s, mostly by cavers from Ukraine and Lithuania."

"Very difficult," added Lasha as he drove. Lasha looked similar to Shurgu, but maybe that's just because they both wore the same kind of sunglasses. Both were broad chested and strong. Lasha had a proper beard rather than a defined mustache and goatee though. "Narrow passages, vertical shafts, and underground chambers. Underwater sections. The Everest of Caves." Both of them spoke English well, but Lasha's accent was a bit harder to understand.

"No one knows how deep it actually goes. You have to climb down several kilometers and then dive in."

I could picture the dark cave, lights shining on deep dark pools of water and I felt excited. This felt good. This felt right.

"Is a very harsh area. Very cold, very humid. Absolutely dark. Most of cave is unexplored. Maybe with drone will be more easy," Shurgu said. He took a long drink of his coffee and tossed the cup onto the floor.

"I climb down too," Lasha said. "Many years ago. Before I meet you. I don't mind cold, I don't mind dark. But I do mind sumps."

Shurgu added, "The flooded tunnels. The reason for scuba gear. Some of these sumps go deep before coming back to air and some go deep and don't come out at all. You must be very careful."

"Interesting," Dante said.

As we drove, the landscape around us changed. We climbed higher into the mountains and here and there were patches of snow on the ground. The mountains rose into the sky with jagged grace, as if they had fought their way out of the earth before coming to a serene halt. There was still a lot of traffic on the road. This was a main highway but it was only two lanes, one going each way, and large trucks took up a lot of space. I could see Mr Thupa ahead of us on his motorbike, but the soldier behind us had fallen back out of sight.

"Once, back in USSR time, a man goes in with his team. Explores for two weeks. Not nice like now. Then you shit where you sleep and sleep where you shit, if you know what I mean. Is dirty work. When he comes out, there is war happening. He almost dies *after* he gets out of cave." Both of the men laughed heartily at this story. I glanced outside. It was growing misty as we climbed higher through the mountains. Touching the window, I could feel the cold seeping in from outside.

"Old story say: this cave is how the Devil roams the earth; he uses Crow Cave to come to and from hell. But cannot be true. Cave is too cold."

Shurgu laughed and looked over to Lasha. But the driver was frowning and his eyes were locked into the rear view mirror. He frowned and grunted at the same time.

"Don't look back. We being followed," Lasha said.

18

A lot of things happened right then. Back through the mist I thought I saw a plume of smoke, but this was forgotten the moment our car skidded out of control. One of the large trucks in front of us turned violently sideways, crashing the hood into the rocky mountainside. It extended backwards, completely blocking the road.

"Shit," Lasha said. He strained at the wheel in an attempt to regain control. "They shoot tires. We must stop."

"Don't worry," Shurgu said. He looked excited as he reached to his waist to pull out his pistol. "They won't fuck with good boys. They not stupid."

It was the last thing he ever said. Three bullets smashed through his window, catching him in the shoulder, the cheek and the throat.

"Shurgu," Lasha cried. Our car came to a halt alongside the highway. We had stopped where an old road intersected the highway. On the left it climbed up into the mountains and on the right it disappeared into the mist. It was from this crossroads that I could see another large truck in the distance behind us, boxing us in. Three black Audis came to a stop about ten meters away. There were no other cars. They had timed their ambush well.

"Get down," Dante said. More bullets riddled our car. *They don't care about saving the map anymore. We are getting too close.* The windows shattered even as the body of the car juddered from the bullets.

"Where the fuck is Mr Thupa?" I snapped.

"Likely dead," Dante said. "Don't worry. I got this."

He unzipped the bag and pulled out a large cassowary shield. It was one of the things I had requested from him, back in Melbourne, but I had never expected to need one like this.

Dante kicked the door open and extended the shield before following it. It was only over a meter and a half tall so he ducked down. Now you may not know what I'm talking about, so let me just pause for a second to explain.

Cassowaries are misunderstood. Yeah, they are real life giant velociraptors with claws that can disembowel a human with as much effort as you'd need to peel a banana. But scary as they look, they're chill as. They don't actually attack, unless heavily provoked. The last time they killed someone was sometime in the 1920s.

That said, their power is terrifying. Even Steve Irwin was bloody terrified of them. When zookeepers approach them, they hide behind large riot shields custom made for protection. It looks like a riot shield from the front, but this one was about ten centimeters thick and weighed at least ten kilograms. It was specifically designed to stop the disemboweling claw from reaching you while also not damaging the cassowary. It just so happened that this also formed a very good protection against bullets. Got it? Good. Now back to that mountainside ambush.

I reached into the duffel bag and pulled out a pistol. Lasha had his gun out and was returning fire by reaching across the dead body of his companion.

The doors to the black cars opened and several men emerged. They had small Uzis cradled to their bodies as they strode through the mist toward us. I clocked their clothing: rustic woolen vests and sheepskin caps. Mountain shepherds perhaps, I thought, but Lasha had an entirely different reaction.

"Boziiish!" he said darkly, using a Georgian curse word that I do not recommend you repeat. "The Shepherds are here? The fucking Shepherds? Shit fuck!"

He dropped his gun on the floor and exited the driver door, holding his hands up. "Surrender," he said. "Don't shoot."

Somewhat surprisingly, they didn't shoot at him. They didn't even seem to notice him. They shot again at Dante. The spray of bullets careened off his shield.

"Give us a hand," he said, sounding as calm as if he unexpectedly needed me to shout him a beer. I reached into the other duffel and withdrew the second shield. It was heavy and I grunted as I passed it out to him.

"I don't think they like you," I said.

"Yeah," he agreed. "I disconcert people."

The advancing men were only five meters away now. Dante shifted, putting his gun down beside me, and then hefted a shield in each hand. He glanced back at me and cocked an eyebrow.

I nodded back at him as I scooped up his gun. He surged forward and I followed, both of us crouching down. I fired with both guns and now the Shepherds were scattering.

I glanced back at our mafia guide but he stood frozen in fear. I would have some questions for him, if we got out of this.

Look, if you have read this far you know I'm pretty hardcore. But I'm not a killer, not unless there is no other option. Even now, which was a life or death situation, I couldn't bring myself to murder those guys. Call it a character flaw. I did shoot the shit out of their hands and legs. Three dropped down and the others fled back to their cars.

There they were met by a very angry Mr Thupa. His face was mangled with road rash, he was limping, but he held a bloody kukri in his hands and he advanced on them with the grim determination of death itself.

I reloaded my pistols as they jumped into one car. It pulled forward and the wounded men climbed in. Within seconds, they had driven back the way we had come.

The air sounded so quiet now that the sound of bullets and screaming had ceased. The only sound was Dante breathing hard as he stood up to his full height. He looked around, taking in the blood stains, the dead man and the coward, and our Gurkha ally.

"Well, stink," Dante said.

"Dantauius Merriweather, you absolute legend." I wanted to drop to the cold road and kiss his feet, but only for a second and if you ever tell him I said that, I'll deny it.

"I apologize, mate."

"Apologize? You just saved our bloody lives!"

"Yeah but I've been calling you some really bad words in my head for making me carry all that junk around. How did you know we'd need bloody cassowary shields?"

I laughed as the euphoria of being alive filled me. "Mate, I thought we'd use them to keep rocks off our heads in Pakistan."

"You're one lucky son of a gun," he said.

"Well we survived. Not everyone did. Let's go check on Mr Thupa. We need to ring his contact back in Tbilisi too. Let him know what went down. And I have some questions for our mafia friend."

"Yeah right," Dante. Then, looking around at the bloody, smoking carnage, he repeated his earlier sentence. "Stink," he said.

19

"Let me being straight with you," Lasha said. "I am not coward." He was driving a white BMW that Mr Thupa had "acquired" for us. It had been a rough two hours. I'll spare you the gory details but they included crawling under the stopped truck with our big bags, my trusty Macpac, our stolen weapons, and our sheer exhaustion. From the far side we heard sirens but getting caught up in a police investigation was not on the menu, even if we *could* trust them to be on the up-and-up.

On the far side of the truck we found a crashed motorcycle, a motorcycle helmet with a nasty dent, and the BMW we now rode in. There had been three dead men in the car, throats cut with a wicked sharp blade. "They almost got me," Mr Thupa said. "But my helmet saved my life. I'm afraid they did get Mr Pun. I'm going to have to tell his wife and kids soon."

"Mate, I'm sorry," Dante began but Mr Thupa, all 160 centimeters of him, held up his hand imperiously. Standing next to Dante he looked like a child telling his father off, but there was nothing funny about him.

"Say no more. Better to die than be a coward. His family will be well taken care of. You will see to that."

He and Lasha had cleaned up the car, Dante had crawled under it and through it, checking for any possible tracking devices, and then we all piled in. We threw our bags in the back seat and kept them unzipped. It didn't seem likely they had another ambush planned but we now all shared the feeling of being hunted.

Despite the danger, I felt excited. If "*they*" (and it bothered me a great deal that I still had no clue who I was up against) had gone through this much trouble, we were close. When someone gets near the top of a mountain and they know they should turn back but they can't, they just keep going even if it's getting dark or a storm is blowing in, they call that summit fever. I had an even worse case of it. I had treasure fever.

So we pressed on, eventually catching up with traffic and leaving that mess far behind. We rode in silence, all of us lost in thought and (presumably) reliving the ambush that we had barely survived. It was then that Lasha had spoken.

"I am not coward," he said. "But every man has limits. Even your superheroes, they know when they are up against someone too strong for them. I am afraid of no man. But I do not fuck with Shepherds. I did not even think they real."

He trailed off as he passed, on a blind turn, a car passing another car. I didn't even feel nervous about this kind of driving anymore, nor would Dante or Mr Thupa.

"He's moving location again," Mr Thupa said. He had been texting on a burner phone. "Mr Rai survived the attack and is moving to Batum—"

"No, don't tell us," I said. "It's better if we don't know."

Mr Thupa waggled his head slightly. "As you prefer. Now that that has been settled, I want to hear more about these shepherds. We have them in Nepal too, wandering from one field to another in the summer sunshine."

"It's not like that," Lasha said. "These not men. They myth. They worship the golden faced witch. Just stories, you know. A man in locked room killed? Must be Shepherd. This secret society of killers, more ancient than assassins. I am not coward. But I not ready to fight monsters from nightmares. I have family."

I considered telling him off, but the truth is he wouldn't have helped much even if he had kept his cool and we had gotten out of the fix without him. It was better for morale to keep him placated.

"Hey," I said. "Happens to the best of us. No worries, mate."

He slowed down a couple of kilometers to find my eyes in the mirror. "I will make up to you. I will make up to you," he said, the mixed relief of being forgiven for a sin you yourself have not forgiven heavy in his voice.

"Assassins. Secret cults. Highway ambushes," said Dante. "It's all a bit much, don't you think?"

'I know," I said. My voice could barely contain my excitement. "What are we going to find on the other end of this? Atlantis?"

Dante snorted but said nothing.

"These Shepherds," I said. "What's the real story? Mountain gangsters with good press? They didn't seem especially fearsome to me."

"You surprise them," Lasha said. "When see them again, they will be angered. Very bad. Very bad."

"And who is the golden faced witch?" Mr Thupa asked.

Lasha did not answer him.

"Some local spirit or legend, no doubt," I said. The existence of a witch or some such nonsense was par for course and didn't trouble me at all. It was not the last thing I would be wrong about.

"We will reach the cave in the next hour," Lasha said. "First we will hike three kilometers up the mountain. There is a trail but it is, how you say, like soap."

"Slippery," I put in.

"Yes, like this. We have heavy packs to carry. Then we reach face of cave."

It took me a second to understand what he meant.

"You mean the mouth?"

"Yes like this. At mouth we go down for three kilometers. Heavy packs. Go slowly. Lots of rope. Scuba gear. But not too heavy or big. Many small places in cave. Can get stuck."

"How long are we going to be down there for?" Dante asked. He sounded a little uncertain, which for him was like another man trembling in fear.

Lasha shrugged as he drove. We couldn't see anything outside of the car through the clouds and the mist and the fog.

"Maybe one week. Maybe two. Cave very big."

"Two weeks," Dante said, and it sounded like he was swearing. "I could really use a drink."

20

And so we did just that. We parked in a muddy field at the base of a mountain with a handful of other vehicles. None of the cars there looked like they had been made after the year 2000. We were in a bit of a jam. Considering we had "acquired" this one from our enemies, we couldn't come back to it. And the cave was too big to bring the large tucker bags in. Even my faithful Macpac wouldn't be able to come with us. We had money and IDs and electronics and visas and other valuables that we couldn't just leave sitting around.

Lasha solved this by arranging to have them transferred to another car. It pulled up twenty minutes after we did and the back was full of ropes, knee pads, wet suits, helmets, headlamps, boots, gloves, water bottles, first aid kits, and scuba gear. The driver puffed on a cigarette in the cold afternoon air as he and Lasha exchanged news in low, terse voices. At one point I heard a phrase that sounded like "Mr Gemsi" and the new driver (I never did catch his name) took a step back. The two men shouted at each other for some time while Dante and I glanced around nervously. Mr Thupa, still splattered in blood and gore, wandered the perimeter. No one else was around on that cold grey day, though I noted a large, ancient yew tree at the center of the car park.

At last we collected and put on the various clothes, equipment and so on. There were also two new packs for us, drybags with straps that were loaded with food and water.

"Where will he go?" I asked Lasha, who shrugged.

"Away," he said. "He come back when I call."

"What if something happens to you?"

"Nothing happens to me."

I thought about mentioning Shurgu, but it didn't seem appropriate. "Let's have a backup plan."

Lasha nodded. He shouted something in Georgian to the driver. That man, who stood only two meters away, shouted back at him. It seemed to take a long time. I glanced over at Dante, but he was busy repacking his pack. At last, the two men concluded their talk.

"If thing happen to me, you meet him in Kutaisi. Go to Golden Fleece monument at 19:00. On Fridays he meet you. Help you."

"Good enough for me." Kutaisi was one of the biggest cities in Georgia and not far from our current location. It was not the firm backup plan I preferred, but under the circumstances it would do. The driver collected everything from us and we waved goodbye to him as he drove off. Mr Thupa went with him, just so I would have my own employee with eyes on our stuff.

Eventually we were alone in the car park. Dante suddenly stood next to me. "You said you explored the cave before?" he said to Lasha. "What can you tell us about it?"

The bearded man explained as we finished packing and began our hike up. The terrain was rocky, with lots of scree and some ice. Our bags were heavy and our progress slow. As we climbed up that mountain, I began to feel like a mouse scurrying away from an owl that watched it with impeccable patience. And hunger. I began to grind my teeth with the frustration of it and the air seemed to grow thick.

Finally Dante grabbed my elbow. "You alright, mate?"

I nodded, then sighed. "Do you feel it?"

"Feel what?"

"Never mind."

"This one of your six sense moments?" he asked.

"I hope not," I said. "I just feel exposed."

"Well, you better appreciate it. Whatever the opposite of exposed is, we're going to feel that for the next week of our lives."

"Constrained? Trapped? Entombed?"

"You're feeling that good about it, eh?" His foot slipped in the gravel but he caught himself.

"Mate," I said, realizing it as I said it. "I wish I'd never seen this bloody map." I know I said I had treasure fever, and I did, but also beneath that was a layer of something like regret but much more profound. There was that old saying that intelligence could be defined as holding two opposing ideas in your head at the same time, and I was really feeling those two ideas stumbling and bumping into one another. Luckily I usually wasn't what you would call a deep thinker, and even this brush with cognitive dissonance left me feeling uneasy.

Dante didn't say anything as we trudged the last bit of the unforgiving ascent. There were three false summits and each time it was heart-breaking to think we had reached the top before seeing how much further we had to go. Here and there we saw litter that spoke of other spelunkers but did not see any other people.

The sun was setting when we finally reached the mouth of the cave. It looked gnarly, like an ancient, hungry mouth of the earth itself. I remembered Lasha saying it was "The Everest of Caves" and I realized with stark appreciation that had been no exaggeration. That said, I later learned that another cave in the area was technically the deepest. I suppose that makes this the K2 of caves, which is still heaps good.

Deeper down there were said to be frozen waterfalls, icy chambers, internal lakes, claustrophobic, often impassable corridors, enormous vertical shafts, and who knew what else. It was the perfect place to hide a treasure. Indeed it was almost too perfect. Even if my treasure map had led me here, it would still be a hell of a time finding whatever lay within. Anything could lie within that otherworldly landscape, including the ones we know about: crustaceans, insects, and the springtail *Plutomurus ortobalaganensis*, aka the deepest living terrestrial animal.

There had been many permits needed and various official permissions from organizations like the Georgian National Speleological Society and the Ukrainian Speleological Association but connections with the mafia have a way of greasing those particular wheels. We were legal and registered, under false names. I had used the name George Georgios, which amused me to no end considering we were in Georgia. Dante went with the boring "Mark Smith," which was so like him.

We had literally several kilometers of rope to use. It lay there, coiled like the world serpent. The thought that we would be that deep in the earth, as deep as that nigh-endless pile of rope, gave me the shivers. Several crows boldly hopped around the ropes and other supplies, cawing in threatening tones. Of course, the cave had been named after these crows, or their ancestors. Voronya Cave means "Crow's Cave" in Ukrainian and had been so named by visiting speleologists from Ukraine. This cave was so big and remote that it had been discovered and named by several different teams over the years.

We kitted up there, putting on our yellow plastic outer layers, our helmets and headlights. Lasha locked in our ropes and then we were ready. I paused, feeling the weight of the pack on my back. The darkness of the cave felt like a song, an absence so powerful that it felt like being punched. There was too much going on now. I took three deep breaths and then turned to my companions.

"Shall we descend into the underworld?"

"Thought you'd never ask," Dante said.

21

I'm not going to lie. I want to get into the details of our abseil down. First of all, it was bad arse. Dante and I of course had our safety certifications. We were veterans of complex vertical caving, low air space caving and we both (okay him especially) were skilled at cave mapping. But we had never gone as deep as this. It sounds cliché, but we really were entering a new world. The massive walls, dark orange in our torch light, stretched all around us as we rappelled down. We were going to be on ropes pretty much the entire time. I was excited again. This shit was what I lived for. So, yeah, I'm champing at the bit (that's the right way to say it, look it up) to explain just how hardcore we were. In many ways, going into deep caves like this is more difficult than high peak mountaineering.

But I get it. SRT (single rope technique) adventures are for a niche audience, so let me just tell you it was an exhilarating, frightening, exhausting experience. With our packs weighing over twenty kilograms, it was hard to keep balance especially in the low light. We kept our lights dim because there was no telling how long the batteries had to last. We had a choice about 200 meters down. The cave divided into two main branches: Non-Kuybyshevskaya (measured to the depth of 1,300 meters) or the Main (measured to the depth of 2,200 meters). If you guessed that we went with option B, congrats. Give yourself a Chupa Chup and a pat on the back.

There were bolts in the caves from past cavers, but otherwise it felt like we were the only people in the world, the only people who had ever lived. It is hard to explain, if you haven't been there dangling on a rope deep in the earth, just how alienating it feels. The wind howled through the chambers, creating eerie echoes. The walls were dripping wet, and we were constantly soaked. Believe it or not, avalanches can happen underground too. It's called breakdown and it's one of my worst fears. Flash flooding is another danger. Even many of the bolts were rusted or dodgy and we had to pause to install new ones.

***

Sump. It's such an innocent little word. It sounds like pump, or chump, or bump: don't be fooled. Sumps are real bastards. Picture deep dark pools of cold water. There's no telling where one ends, and you have to stop and spend ages switching to your scuba gear to get through. Even in a wetsuit you can feel the cold water pressing in all around you, and then sometimes the cave grows narrow, like it's trying to close in and grab you. Some of them are deep, too, forty or fifty meters deep. That might not sound like a lot, but trust me: in the dark, at the bottom of the world, every meter is a struggle. Navigating sumps is by far the most dangerous part of spelunking.

How long did we travel for? Fuck me, it felt like ages. Eventually, after having gone through three sumps we unclipped from the ropes at last and found the remnants of an old camp. It must have been recent because the damp and the dark quickly erased all leftovers of humanity. Lasha told us there could be as many as five, though it was anyone's guess how many were left. He also informed us that we had already gone further than he had on his previous visit. I didn't like hearing that. We ate and spoke in low voices and slept for far too short of a time.

I awoke in the dark, momentarily unsure of where I was. The recent events came back to me like a bad dream. Only it was worse than a bad dream. It was a bad reality. I felt a pressure in my bladder and got up to relieve myself.

The other two men were sleeping so I turned my headlamp on the dimmest setting and stumbled a reasonable distance down the cave. There are some cavers who do their business in bags and bring them back up but I figure I'm just adding to the nature. I had just about finished when I glanced to the left and saw them. Wet footprints. They were coming from deeper into the cave. A chill that had nothing to do with the cold ran down my spine.

I ran back to the others. My heavy footsteps woke them and I found them both sitting up and staring.

"There's other people down here with us," I said, and told them about the footprints. We all rushed to examine them. One was just barely visible now, but we turned up our lights and saw the trail that led from and to the deeper parts of the cave. It felt like someone had stepped out of the distant past to come watch us in our sleep. It was an ominous, chilling feeling.

"This not good," said Lasha.

"Interesting," Dante said.

I thought about the assassin who had dogged my steps since the day I got the map. (Or the team of assassins or whatever.) But surely they wouldn't be coming from inside the cave. And they would have killed us in our sleep, I supposed. So that was the good news. It wasn't an assassin who had padded up in the darkness to watch us while we slept. The bad news was, obviously, that we had no idea who it could be. Cavers we didn't know about, perhaps, but this would be strange behavior on their part.

We couldn't go back to sleep after that, even though according to our watches it was just after 4 in the morning. We kept going, a bit more slowly today. We clipped back into ropes, and followed the footsteps.

Everything was going swimmingly until we had to go swimming. We switched to our scuba gear, put our rucksacks into dry bags, and set up our backup oxygen supply to use if a fault developed with our 'rebreather' apparatus.

The dive started off as planned, as we navigated our way through the narrow underwater caves. At a few points I worried about getting through, and was amazed that Dante made it. His massive frame, usually such an asset, was here a major detriment. I supposed that was true of all advantages. In different contexts, they could become a disadvantage. That was interesting but I didn't have time to dwell on it. I pushed ever down in the pitch blackness.

There was no communication other than hand signals and simple signs clumsily made with our gloved hands. After more than two and a half hours, I was deep in my zone and slightly worried about running out of oxygen. Our small tanks only held three hours of air. That was when Dante tugged on my shoulder. He indicated something urgently.

I had no idea what he meant. I shrugged the best I could. *What?* He grabbed his own arms and hugged himself. He jerked his thumb behind him and held up three fingers before dropping one. *Two*. He hugged himself again, then did the same thing with his fingers. I looked behind him, above him and my heart skipped a beat.

I was slowly piecing together what he was saying. *Two not three. Hugged. No. Held. No. Trapped.* Lasha was not here. The poor man was trapped.

22

Hey! It's me, the nephew again. I just realized that you might not know much about Lasha Dzidziguri. Uncle Jad had met him before and so didn't give him much description. I've checked some of his old photos and journal entries not connected to this story to provide a bit more detail.

Lasha looked to be in his late 40s, with salt-and-pepper hair slicked back, an immaculately groomed mustache. In photos taken in the city, he wore a tailored three-piece suit in deep jewel tones (emerald, burgundy, navy) paired with dark leather gloves. Of course, he had plenty of gold rings, a chunky watch, and a cane with a wolf's head handle. Despite his refined fashion, he had a noticeable knife scar along his jaw (and apparently on his stomach) and a tattoo of St. George slaying the dragon on his forearm. In this story, he was dressed more simply and then covered in diving equipment, but it's important to remember, I think, that he was completely out of his element and yet always gave his full effort.

He was the kind of guy to send Georgian poetry as an esoteric warning to his enemies before escalating the issue. Like many of his countrymen, he believed every meal should be a proper feast, and he was notorious for refusing to do business in a place that served bad khinkali. I don't have a complete idea of his branch of expertise, but I definitely caught references to smuggling, gambling, and "protection" rackets mainly in the Ponichala neighborhood of Tbilisi. His favorite food? Grilled lamb, naturally, and as an Aussie I approve of that.

The last detail I found was my favorite. In his twenties, he carried around a pet ferret named Bebo, because "Bebo is a better judge of character than most men."

I often feel that way about my dog, so I totally see where Lasha is coming from. Anyway, sorry for the interruption. Let's get back to it.

23

Dante and I swam back up the cave together. It seemed to take forever, though probably it was less than five minutes. Lasha was easy to see as he struggled and bobbed in his bright yellow rubbers. He flashed his light on and off in a series of three short, three long, and three short blinks. *SOS.* With our air growing short we had to get him out quickly.

I looked around. This had been one of the areas that had troubled me. The cave tunnel was narrow here, almost like a shoot or slide. Sharp stone protrusions, like mini-stalactites, extended from the ceiling. He had gone low but then got squeezed in by the narrow sides. I looked at Dante, even though I couldn't see his face. Lasha was really wedged in there. He had clearly panicked and made things worse.

I checked my watch. Thirteen minutes of air left. I thought we were close to the end of the sump, but there was no guarantee. But I would not, could not leave this man to drown here, even if it meant I had to join him in an unmarked, underwater grave. The second rule of tomb raiding is: you never leave a man behind.

It wasn't going to come to that, however. The first problem was communication. *Next time we need earpieces,* I thought. We had brought so much stuff but I had somehow overlooked this necessity. I turned my lamp to its most dim setting so that I didn't blind the poor bloke. Then I swam up to him and extended my hands. He reached out and I grabbed his hands. The black gloves gave me a loose grip but I pulled as hard as I could. Dante saw what I was doing and swam up to Lasha's right arm. He pulled there, and I used all my strength while holding the left hand.

Nothing. Three minutes had passed. Well, I hadn't thought it would be that easy but we had to try. If we could get around him, a push might work better but of course he completely blocked the cave.

I pride myself on my quick thinking and, honestly, if you have come this far with me you can see why. So hopefully you can understand my terror: we faced an anonymous death deep underground but what really frightened me was that I had no idea what to do. We had eight minutes left, and needed at least a few of those to reach air again.

I thought about what Nova might have said. "Just chill out, boss," I heard in her voice, which didn't really help. But I did feel a little more relaxed, at least until I looked at my watch and saw we had six minutes left. Okay, no more time left for thinking.

I pointed at Lasha and held my hands up in an attempt to tell him to *be ready*. Then I swam back away from him and then towards him as fast as I could. I hit him hard, or as hard as could be underwater. I swear he moved back at least thirty centimeters. But he was still jammed in there. Four minutes. We would have to leave, change tanks and come back for him. Hopefully he could last. As I considered this, Dante pushed me aside and then did his own swim/slam. It moved Lasha back another sixty centimeters or so.

We're going to do this! I thought. But I glanced at my watch and I saw our time.

Four minutes left of air.

Shit.

I swam again, at a weird angle but there was no time. I slipped past Dante and hit Lasha in his chest. There was a cracking sound. He moved back though and I moved with him. He was free! I smiled beneath my mask and then realized what that cracking sound had been. The hose had busted off my oxygen tank. We had to go through the tight cave gap once more. He went first, more carefully and a little higher and made it. I was on his heels. Dante was already at the edge of the chamber. When he saw us, he blinked the light at us. Long short short short. Short long short. Then long short short short. Despite the fact that I was holding my breath, I almost laughed as I translated his blips.

BRB.

Something light shone down upon me and I looked up. We had somehow opened a door or panel in the ceiling. I swam up to it and saw that it looked manmade. The rough stone walls had been hewn into a facsimile of smoothness. Not far above was light, and that meant, hopefully air.

I motioned to Dante, who was watching me, waiting for my signal. *Come here,* my hand signal said. He did so and, upon seeing the sky tunnel, swam up into it immediately. Even as he did so, the last of my oxygen fled. I took a deep breath and we all swam up.

Lasha swam ahead of me. He didn't know I was out of air, and he had less than two minutes himself. I swam at a relaxed pace, conserving air even as panic grew within me. My lungs began to burn and I grew lightheaded.

We reached the light maybe thirty seconds later, but it felt like a lifetime. I emerged from the dark pool even as the last air exploded out of my lungs. We had made it! We sat on a large stone floor. Above us, a kilometer or two above, a bit of light came in from the ceiling. It was a thin and sickly light that barely reached us, to be sure, but down here it felt almost like staring into a torch.

There was no time to celebrate. Dante was already midway through changing his tank. Behind him was a jagged imposing archway half hidden beneath an overhang. A rusted steel gate blocked further egress. I thought of the person who had watched us. Had they come from here?

Dante was staring at my broken apparatus. "Far out," he said. "Your tank is totally munted."

"Yeah," I said, taking off my mask. I couldn't hide my smile. "I almost died."

He started laughing, his deep peels filling the cavern.

I started laughing too and couldn't stop. "I almost died, mate."

"You almost died," he echoed.

I might still be there laughing, except I glanced over to Lasha. His stone-faced glower showed only concern at being saddled with two maniacs.

I caught my breath and finished removing my underwater gear.

"Where the hell are we?" I asked.

"I'll have to check our records," Dante said. "But I think it's safe to say we're off the charts." He opened up his dry bag as Lasha and I slipped out of our wetsuits. By the time we had changed, he came over and we pored over the charts and maps. We had emerged into an uncharted world.

We wandered over to the gate and looked at it. It looked old, but not ancient. It was, as I had said, rusting in the damp air, but it stood strong. There was no obvious lock or moving mechanism to get inside, but the door behind it. That looked proper old. And the rest of the cave lay behind it. We wandered back to our stuff. I was thinking about swimming back down to close the hidden panel we had found, just in case we were being followed, but then I looked up and saw Dante staring at me. I realized he had asked me something and we were sitting in the stink of an unanswered question like a fart after curry night.

"Eh?" I asked.

"The map," he said. "Let's have a look."

I recoiled, feeling like a wolf protecting my food from mangy scavengers. But I caught myself. "Reckon it's time," I agreed. "Let's have a bite and a drink."

Lasha cooked up some noodles on our camping stove and Dante pulled out a couple of Coopers. This is not a wise investment in terms of weight but we justified it for our mental health. We had a geez at the ancient paper. Something caught my attention. The part of the marginalia around the edge near the cave stood out. A double axe sat above a griffon sat above a word.

I pointed it out to Dante. He studied it for a long moment. I could smell the instant noodles cooking and my stomach rumbled.

"The monster means protection, maybe divine protection. Double axe means royalty or king," he said. "The word looks Minoan, but I can't read the Greek."

"It's not Greek," I said, with the enthusiasm of a nerd who knows an obscure fact. I was impressed but not surprised by his deep knowledge. He had had a great teacher, after all. "It's Lycian. They were a people who lived in modern Southern Turkey eventually swallowed up by the Macedonians. They used the labrys too," I said, nudging the double axes with my fingernail.

"Interesting. So what's it say?"

"Well that's a good question. I know the word but it's hard to translate. Maybe Middle English comes closest with dweomer."

"What's that?"

I rolled up the map and looked up at his eyes. He wasn't going to like this. "Magic," I said.

24

"Come on now," Dante said. He looked uncomfortable.

"Mate, I'm not saying that there is magic. But it's something that they, the mapmakers, believed in. Or something they pretended to have for their power. It means that we can probably open that gate using some kind of trick. That still a problem?"

He didn't so much shake his head as tilt it slightly. "Yeah nah."

Dante really didn't like the idea of esoteric things. He would leave the room when Nova and I would read each other our horoscopes. The suggestion of creatures such as ghosts or angels and such made him furious. Like any intelligent person, I also didn't go for such obvious bunk, but it amused me how far his dislike went. He almost took it personally, like magic itself had hurt him when he was a child.

We ate our noodles and finished our beers. Lasha had been silent but now he spoke.

"Again, I thank you. You saved my life."

Ah, so that was the deal. He still was feeling survivor's guilt.

"Think nothing of it, mate," I said magnanimously. "You found the hidden door, after all."

"Makes me wonder how many hidden doors we already missed," Dante said. That idea was staggering. These vast caverns could hold thousands of hidden chambers. I felt overwhelmed and roused. What hidden treasures there must be! It would require a small army, working in tandem. I pictured the chambers, full of people, tapping away at all the surfaces and realized it was better to leave some secrets hidden. (As long as I could get my hands on this one.)

Dante was pacing. It wasn't easy, as the length of rock between the pool of water and the locked gate was no more than four meters, but he made it work. Lasha, for his part, was resting against the cold stone wall. This, despite all that had happened these last couple of days, restored my confidence in him. The sign of an old campaigner was someone who knew when to grab some sleep when they could.

I rose and met Dante mid stride. "Shall we?" I asked. It says something, now that I think about it, that he didn't even have to specify. He knew what was up. We set to work, certain we could unlock the so-called magic of this gate.

In case there was a voice recognition system with pre-set commands, I shouted "Open Sesame!" as well as words like "password,"

123456789," "dragon," "monkey," and "shadow." These are just some of the most common passwords. (Other popular passwords include words like "superman," "starwars," "6969," and "matrix." These are things you have to know in my profession.) I tried them in English, Russian, Greek, Aramaic, Latin, and Sanskrit, moving around to different locations in the chamber. Finally I was confident that either there was no voice recognition or that I couldn't crack it.

Meanwhile, Dante checked for concealed pressure plates. He dropped down and checked for motion sensors and plates near the gate. He then checked every wall and every floor piece, save for where Lasha slept.

We checked in with each other with a glance and took a quick break to eat our noodles and finish our beers. Then it was time to get moving again. I broke open my backup compass and pulled out the magnet. It had occurred to me that, if attached to a wand or stick, some ancient wizard could trigger a magnetic lock hidden in the gate. Nothing.

Dante used a flashlight to reflect light in case it was that kind of solution. He tried a dozen different angles and then a dozen more. Meanwhile I moved on from magnets and checked for a heat sensor. I snapped open a hotpack and checked the gate and then the floor and the walls.

"It's interesting," Dante said as I walked up to him.

"It's not usually this hard," I said. "But remember that underground chamber in Riga? Took us two days. Reckon we'll do better here."

He nodded. "I'll check for anything mechanical." He moved on to see if any part of anything could twist or be moved. This could reveal any hidden buttons or fake rocks as well.

I began to wonder just how ancient the gate was. Maybe that was part of the trick, that it was newer than it looked. There could be RFID or NFC tech at work here. I pulled out my burner phone and turned it on. Meanwhile Dante continued to check for moving parts. He even dipped his arms deep into the water, which was a good idea. I hadn't thought about that, and I should have.

We spent another hour trying everything we could think of. Thinking of possible radiation, I checked my Gamma watch, which had a tiny built-in Geiger counter. There was no sign of anything worrisome. Finally I sighed loudly and crouched down next to Lasha.

"I'm knackered," I said to Lasha.

He smiled at me. Why not? He'd just had a good long nap. "Old Georgian folk tale about Little Thief. He sing a song and his boots fill with money. Every day he do this, and his boots are very full. So much money he must dig in earth to hide it all."

Honestly I was only half listening, distracted by the urgent issue of whether or not it was too early to cook more instant noodles. But something he had said took root.

"What? You mean we could try singing?" I said. "I already tried it. I said pretty much everything that anyone could think of...."

I trailed off. Was it possible that singing, humming, or playing a tune on an instrument could create a special kind of vibration? Such a thing had never occurred to me. It seemed far-fetched at best, but then so did all good ideas at first. And considering where we were: literally far below the surface of the earth, it wasn't so crazy.

I leapt to my feet with new energy. "Lasha, mate, you're a bloody genius."

"I only tell story," he protested.

I walked up to the gate. Dante joined me, his arms and hands dripping cold water.

"No luck," he said.

"One more thing to try," I said. "If it doesn't work, we can go back in the water and come up somewhere else." Neither of us liked that idea. We were in a secret passage. It must lead somewhere. But both of us had been in similar passages without any payoff. We knew the score. I thought about how to explain this and gave up pretty quickly. I was good at using my words, of course, but some situations are explanation proof, and this was one of them.

"Just, uh, bear with me, eh?"

I stood there, about a meter away from the gate, and belted out "Yesterday. All my troubles seemed so far away." I wasn't a great singer, but I didn't embarrass myself at karaoke nights.

Dante narrowed his eyes but said nothing. I hadn't thought my first song would work anyway.

"What's the oldest song you can think of?" I asked him.

"Some hymn or ballad."

That was a good idea. Georgia was a thoroughly Christian nation.

"Amazing Grace. How sweet the sound," I sang. My voice sounded good. Caves made for good acoustics. But nothing happened.

I had to assume that the gate was modern or at least relatively so. If a song was required, and it was something circa 800 BCE, then we were shit out of luck. But I had the feeling that it wasn't.

I tried Beethoven, Bach, Grieg, and Vivaldi, chanting and humming and whistling several of the obvious tunes. Then inspiration struck. "Oi, Lasha," I called. "What's your national anthem? Hang on. Come on over and give us a listen."

The bearded man was apparently growing immune to our eccentric methods. He sat there packing his bag but when I called him he trotted over.

"Song is Tavisupleba. Is very important for us. I once sing to fascist skinheads at punk bar. They stab here and here." He pulled up his shirt and revealed two sullen scars.

He sang for a bit, and then a bit more and then I stopped him.

"Is good?" he asked.

"Yeah, is good," I said, despondently. I was falling into the trap of wanting it to work. But it hit me. Georgia was a new country. Well this incarnation of it was new. "Hang on. How long has this been your anthem?"

"Twenty years. Is very popular song. Everyone sing it to President Bush when he visit. Old song is very boring."

"Can you sing that one?" I asked, trying and I think mostly succeeding at hiding my excitement. I looked over at Dante. He still looked skeptical. This would change his tune (no pun intended,) I was sure of it.

Lasha sang loudly and off-key but proud as could be. The words were something like "Praise be to heavenly Bestower of Blessings, Praise be to paradise on earth," and so on.

Nothing happened.

"Mother of pearl," I swore. I was so filled with disappointment that I could taste it, like bile, at the back of my throat.

"Thanks Lasha," I said. "You did great."

He went back to his station while I stared at that damn gate.

Dante put his arm around me. "Hey, good time or good story, right?"

It was then I realized what a fool I had been. He was going to be taking the piss out of me for years now. I could see him there in the pub, holding court to a table full of our friends. *"And then old Jad bloody started singing to the gate. I thought he was going to bloody propose."*

Well I suppose I deserved it. But I must have looked real despondent, because he double cheered me up.

"You know what she would have said. You can't always get what you want."

The words bypassed my brain and went straight through my mouth. "You can't always get what you want," I sang loudly, in a decent Mick Jagger impression. I put my hand on my heart in a reflexive pose of heartfelt passion. But I was thinking of Nova. She had been a Stones fan, but more importantly an unabashed singer of this song whenever things even slightly didn't go her way. "But if you try sometime, you just might find, yeah, you get what you need."

As I finished, the gate clicked and swung open.

Dante's jaw dropped. That's not an expression. It actually opened as wide as possible.

"Far out," he said.

25

The door behind the gate opened without a hitch, but we did not enter right away. Without really talking about it, we dressed as if for battle. This was the mythic underworld and as the heroes we needed to be proper kitted up. The inside of the cave was dry and horizontal. I considered leaving our heavy scuba gear here but dismissed it. We didn't know what lay ahead and it was possible we wouldn't return this way. Besides, if there were midnight stalkers, we didn't want to leave our stuff vulnerable to their mischief. It was sound logic, but my back regretted it.

We also brought the rope. Not to rappel now, not this time, but as our thread to find our way through and (more importantly) back through this labyrinth. Theseus's gift from Ariadne. So we went slowly, and only after first tying the end of the rope into a piton we hammered into the floor.

We went through the door and entered the tunnel. The air felt different here. Warmer, yes, but more still. Old. No, strike that. Ancient. This tunnel looked hewn out of the earth too. It reminded me of Petra or Cappadocia, except that here bioluminescent fungi clinging to the walls, casting ghostly green and blue glows.

We hadn't gone more than three minutes when we entered a large chamber. We walked with the considered quiet deliberateness of cat burglars. We were intruders: we could feel that in our bones.

This room raised my hackles. There were remnants of modern activity: abandoned mining equipment, reinforced steel doors, and broken halogen lights. But on the wall above the door across from us, hung a golden mask that hazily gleamed in our low torchlight. It was the face of a woman and it hung about four meters above the floor.

"Golden witch," Lasha said, crossing himself.

"Eh,' I said. "All cults have leaders. You can't expect them to call her 'Lucy from accounting' or whatever that unpleasant person really does."

I was trying to boost his spirits (mine as well, truth be told) but my voice was thin and uncertain. That mask was creepy. The eyes felt like they were watching us, and her face though human looked somehow uncanny valley. Was it less than human or more human than human? I couldn't tell, no matter how long I stared.

"Equipment looks Soviet," Dante said to me.

"Huh," I said, although that made a kind of sense. They would have had the resources and ruthless willpower to get people down here.

"Does that mean they built this?" I asked.

Dante half shrugged. He wasn't one to pull out a theory or supposition before it had been fully baked.

"Not Soviet," Lasha said. "This old. Very old. Gold witch very old."

"Will you shut up about the golden—"

I stopped. The eyes on the mask had grown slightly bigger, like they were dilating in our light. Hadn't they?

"Did anyone else see that?" I asked.

"See what?" Dante asked.

I almost didn't say anything, out of fear of being ridiculous. But I would rather be too paranoid than not enough.

"I thought the eyes moved. Or got bigger maybe."

"The eyes? On the mask?" Dante asked. "Far out." His tone was dismissive and annoyed but I persisted.

"Just keep an eye on it," I said. "No pun intended."

The large chamber we were in had several doors. The biggest one lay directly under the golden mask, so we examined the others first. Behind the first two were old, moldering sleeping cots. They must have dated to the Soviet times. One of them had a human skeleton atop it. We didn't examine it that closely. The rooms had a funky smell, like mildew and void.

One of the doors just wouldn't open. Another seemed to be a latrine, which made sense. Luckily the smell had long ago receded. As we searched, I became ever more aware of a constant hum so faint it almost seemed like my imagination.

"Do you hear that?" I asked Dante in a low tone.

He listened carefully. "No," he said. "Hang on. Some ventilation system maybe?"

There was nothing strange about what he said, but I shivered. We stood under the main chamber under the basilisk gaze of that golden mask.

A thought occurred to me but I dismissed it. We went to work, asking Lasha to simply watch the tunnel we had come through. Most GPR (that's ground-penetrating radar to those of you not in the biz) is huge, as big as a lawnmower. But I had a handheld prototype about the size of an electric drill. I used it to check for hidden basements or hidden chambers. Dante did something similar with portable seismic sensors. He checked every nook and every cranny of every room, looking for changes in density.

I had some other goodies in my bag but they weren't needed here. Time passed as I was absolutely absorbed. The fact that we found nothing didn't even phase me. This was us in our element.

The thought came back. I shook my head.

"What's wrong?" Dante asked.

"Nothing, mate," I said. We continued our search. Some of the chambers off the main room went back deeper than it first looked. There were rusted old lockers at the back of one of them but they were empty of all save for dust and cold emptiness.

At last there was only the skeleton. I glanced at my gloves, making sure they hadn't ripped or torn and then stripped the blanket. The skeleton looked exactly like you'd expect. I scanned it on a whim but there was nothing special. Those eyes. I felt the blanket carefully, thinking something could have been sewn in.

I stopped and walked over to Dante. The urge had grown too strong and I was thinking about the third rule of tomb raiding: there will always be something to steal. He looked up at me from where he squatted on the floor. His eyes were a question. "Dante, mate," I said. "Boost me up. I'm going to steal the mask."

26

So there I stood, on Dante's broad shoulders like a chump. I reached out for the mask and it was as though the air thickened around it. I had to make an effort to move my hands. My left boot slipped a bit as I strained.

"Easy," Dante said. He had his hands braced on the wall. Lasha watched us with a mix of wonder and fear. I struggled through the heavy air but reached the mask. The eyes of the mask looked at me like, "What are you going to do now, tough guy?"

With a shocking amount of effort, I got my gloved hands on the mask. It burned through the thick material. Did those eyes look triumphant at that point? I want to say yes but it was such a split second impression. I gasped and slipped right off Dante, falling two meters to the ground, twisting mid-air to land hard on my shoulder.

I barely felt the fall. My hands still burned. "It burns," I said.

Dante's face appeared so close to mine. "It's hot?" he asked.

"No, cold," I said. "So cold."

Lasha was next to me too. "Big fall. You alright?"

"Yes," I said. "I'll live." I got to my feet and stretched out my arms. I'd be bruised but it had been more embarrassing than painful. "Think we can leave that mask there though."

"Cold, you said," Dante mused. "There must be something feeding it. A current or something behind it."

I pulled off my gloves, thinking my fingers would be black with frostbite or something, but they looked fine. "Let's forget the bloody mask," I said.

Dante didn't say anything but his posture spoke of pure disagreement. "Worth a lot of money," he said. "Maybe some old tech."

"Well you're welcome to try. I don't recommend it."

He stared up at the mask for three long seconds, then sighed. "I suppose you know best."

"I usually do," I agreed. For once, though, I wasn't so sure. *What had we gotten into?*

We left the one door unopened against our best wishes, and finally opened the last unopened door, the one below the mask. Slowly we went into the next room. It looked just like the previous one except it was about eighty percent smaller. The air was cold and damp, carrying the scent of wet stone. There was no equipment in this one, but the same side rooms. No golden mask hanging like a sun in the sky, and that was strangely a relief. It felt less oppressive here. We got to work, and Lasha even got involved.

The time went quickly for me and in truth my mind was still on that mask. But instead of greed, I felt the first stirrings of dread and fear. The two-and-a-half hours passed quickly but we eventually assessed that the room and adjoining rooms held no surprises. Thus assured we sat and ate some churchkhela to replenish our strength. (Churchkhela is sort of like a Georgian lolly, made by dipping strings of walnuts, hazelnuts, or almonds into a thickened grape juice mixture. It looks and sort of tastes like eating a purple candle but a little sugar comes in handy.)

Thus fortified, we ventured through the big door at the far end. Another room, this one seemingly as big as the first awaited us. This chamber had a disused reactor in its center, covered in mineral deposits, as if nature had been hard at work for several decades reclaiming it. A faint, flickering red emergency light cast long shadows.

I didn't like this room. It felt like I was hearing strange echoes, faint whispers, distant mechanical sounds: distorted sounds that disappeared when I stopped to listen for them. I again felt like I was a prey, scurrying about beneath sharp claws that I could not see.

Again we took out our tools and searched. After an hour, all of our headlamps pulsed off, only for a few seconds and then turned back on. That darkness was complete. If your only experience with darkness has been at night, above ground, beneath the stars, you have no idea what true darkness is like. You can put your hand a centimeter away from your face and not see it. It's maddening, in a way. The lights came back on a few seconds later, but it felt like an eternity in the darkness.

"What the hell was that?" I asked, looking at the two of them. Lasha looked like he could barely hold it together.

"This I don't know," Lasha said.

Dante too looked unhappy. "Electromagnetic pulse?" he said. His tone indicated how unlikely he thought that was.

"That's not really how it works," I said. "We've got triple A batteries in these."

"Fluke then?" Dante suggested.

"I don't like flukes, Dante," I said sternly. "You know I don't."

But nothing like that happened again and we resumed our search. I did pick up faint radiation with my Gamma watch, but it was at a level of interest, not concern. This time we might have been a little more cursory, but it still required almost two hours of concentration before we were ready to move on to the next room.

"I guess another smaller room is coming up," I said as we stood before the door. That had been the pattern so far. Big room, smaller room, big room, smaller room. What did that remind me of?

Dante opened the door, and as we stepped through, I realized two things. This room was enormous, with wings that stretched away to the right and the left. It created a half moon that was easily five or six times larger than the rooms we had explored already. All that was secondary though.

The main thing I noticed was it was crawling with giant, pale fuck-off spiders the size of ponies. As our dim lights entered their chamber, their heads swung toward us revealing a complete lack of eyes. The chittering started even as the heavy door behind us swung shut. My Gamma watch started clicking like crazy.

"Well, stink," Dante said.

"And here I thought we had big ones in Australia," I said. "Lasha, mate, what is up with these?" I was not fully surprised though, because I was aware of the art of tomb raiding. The fourth rule of tomb raiding is this: something will want to kill you.

"These not normal Georgia spiders," Lasha protested. We braced ourselves as the spiders surged toward us with ugly arachnid urgency.

27

Hi, it's me again. The nephew here. I know that the next part feels like some kind of adventure novel. I mean … giant spiders? Come on! So I checked on this with the science department at La Trobe, not saying much other than enquiring about how underground spiders might evolve. I have to admit I was hoping they would tell me it was complete nonsense. But they didn't. Not exactly. Here's a copy of the response I got back from Dr. Darelle Klab.

Spiders that evolve deep beneath the earth, in an environment with no light, would likely develop a range of adaptations suited for survival in total darkness. Since there's no need for camouflage or UV protection, these spiders would likely be albino or translucent, allowing them to blend with cave walls or avoid detection from predators. In pitch-dark environments, vision is useless, so their eyes might shrink, disappear, or become highly specialized for detecting faint bioluminescent signals. To better navigate rocky surfaces and sense vibrations, they could develop extra-long legs and hyper-sensitive hairs to detect movement and air currents. Some species might evolve bioluminescence to lure prey or communicate, glowing softly in the dark like deep-sea creatures.

Instead of traditional webs, they might create funnel-like burrows or massive underground snares, using vibration-sensitive silk to detect movement. Or one supposes they could become ambush predators, relying on stealth and ultra-sensitive limbs to detect passing prey. Since vision is unnecessary, they might develop extreme sensitivity to pheromones and chemical trails to locate prey in the darkness. With prey in the deep underground being limited, one might speculate that they would evolve a highly potent venom to quickly immobilize scarce food sources. I could go on but those are the first things that occur to me.

I am curious as to your letter. It did not read as idle speculation to me. Even here in the gated community of academia the name Jad Malek is not unknown. Has your family discovered some new species? One trembles at the thought (not to mention the grant money). Let me know.

Yours,
Dr. Klab

I never responded to him. What could I have said? But his description about my innocuous question was eerily similar to Uncle Jad's. The only thing he didn't mention was their preposterous size, and with the nuclear radiation down there, that wasn't a shock. So who knows what happened? Take it as embellishment if you want to. I wish I still could.

28

"Crikey," I said. "Look at the size of the unpleasant persons." I dropped to my knees and whipped my backpack off my back. "Buy me a few seconds, mate."

Dante glanced down at me and then moved to stand in front of me. I put my hand in the bag, looked up, and froze.

I don't think I fully realized how horrific these creatures were. The tops of their bodies were almost two meters high. Their legs were long, and disturbingly hairy, going up past two meters before coming down to the ground. Their skin (do spiders have skin?) was pale and translucent. Their faces had no eyes, which was somehow the worst thing about them. It made them look like aliens.

Correction. The worst thing about them was their slavering mouths. I'm not one of those blokes afraid of spiders. I don't mind a Huntsman in my garden. As a teen, I'd been bitten by a redback and rushed to hospital for the anti-venom and it didn't leave any scar. Well, not any emotional ones anyway. My little toe was another matter. But the size of these creatures disturbed me in a profound way. What did they even live on down here? How had they gotten so large? The answer occurred to me on the heels of the question. *Radiation.*

Dante pulled the rock hammer from his belt. This had been designed in some Swiss lab to put pitons into walls, not to pulverize giant spiders. But he made do. The first three spiders reached him, chittering into the darkness. Though they didn't have eyes, they seemed to sense the light somehow. More importantly, they seemed to dislike or distrust it.

Dante smashed into one with the hammer. It withdrew silently, leaking fluids, but there were dozens more waiting to take its place. The one on Dante's left tried to bite down with its fangs (or whatever you call those sharp things spiders have) but Dante punched it with his left hand. He hit it hard enough that its legs crumbled and it sank to the floor.

I looked away. Lasha had pulled out his gun but even as he raised it I held up my hand. "Not yet," I said. Gunshots were not that loud, in the overall scheme of things, but the only thing I could imagine worse than death by giant spiders was death by cave-in.

"Then do what?" he asked. "What else I have?"

"Do what I do," I said. I pulled junk out of my enormous pack. The snacks and exploratory gear were on top but I tossed them to the ground like so much refuse. I cut the ropes we had and threw the excess loops on the floor. Finally I found what I was looking for.

Three magnesium flares. We carried these for two reasons: emergency signaling devices or as a light source in extreme need. Well, our need was extreme and these things would burn at a temperature over 1,600 degrees.

"Eyes," I called out in warning. The other two covered their eyes. I did too as I lit it, thinking of cartoon characters using TNT as weapons. My eyes were closed and my hand was over them but as I lit it, it was like someone threw the sun into my face. The intense light was stunning, a vibrant assault so ferociously bright I felt like I might spew. The heat coming off was intense as well, so I lobbed first one, then two, then all three flares toward the mass of giant spiders.

The smell of burnt hair and angry chittering made me want to open my eyes but it was impossible. We had adjusted to total darkness so this light was intense, like staring at a thousand eclipses. But the noise and the smell of the spiders receded and the sizzle of the flare was prominent in our ears.

"Dante, mate," I said. I realized my voice was needlessly loud. "How's it look?"

"Bugger if I know," he said. "I'm swinging my hammer and not hitting anything, so we seem okay."

"Lasha, mate. How you going?"

"This very fucked," Lasha said. Though his English wasn't perfect, he had a talent for putting things just the right way.

We all knew the flare would last ten, fifteen minutes tops. It was a long wait, made so much worse as the sounds of new spiders drew newer. Their scuffling feet and chittering mouths were too awful, and I could not bear it anymore. I opened my eyes and the brightness gave me a migraine.

I immediately wanted to close them again but made a mental effort to resist the urge. I was staring at a sea of spiders. Instead of dozens, there were hundreds. Probably not thousands if I'm being honest, but to me right then it felt like thousands. We were, you'll remember, at the entrance of an enormous chamber. Each way I looked, until the room disappeared into shadows, there were large spiders coming towards us. The sight of them was bad, but their smell? Like a rotting body dipped in vinegar.

I moved back to the door. It had slammed shut when we entered but if we could get it open, move back into the last room, and close the door, we'd be safe from the spiders. Then we could figure out our next step (which right then felt like getting the hell out of the caves).

Dante must have opened his eyes then because I heard him say, "Mother of pearl." Even as I fiddled with the door, I glanced back at

Dante. He stood behind the flares, a hammer dripping ichor in his hand. With the red flames behind him, he looked like a hero out of Greek mythology. The nearest spiders stopped at the three flares but they could go around them. I had thrown them blindly and not too precisely.

"Light more," I called as I fumbled again with the door. There was no handle, no latch. I saw no hinges. It was a stone door that had sunk back into the stone. No doubt there must be a lever somewhere to open it, but hell if I knew where it was.

I heard the soft murmur of prayer, and knew without looking where it came from. Poor Lasha. He was a powerful man in his city and his country, but anyone taken this much out of their comfort zone would struggle.

Dante appeared beside me. The flares were three meters ahead of us and beginning to burn down. One spider drew closer. Others were fanning out and coming in from the sides.

"Any luck?" he asked.

I hit the door with my palm and shook my head. "We might need a plan B."

He nodded. "It's been a minute since I took chemistry, but I have an idea."

It took me a few moments to guess at his meaning.

"Oh. Yeah, go for it, mate," I said, thinking how nice it would be to have those cassowary shields. At least we had our helmets. "Lasha, come here. And get behind your backpack. Put your head down, helmet up."

The Georgian man did so, giving me a quizzical look as Dante pulled a Nalgene full of water out of his backpack. We crouched down and waited.

The spiders, in a mass of pale hairy legs and slavering jaws, came forward. They sensed dinner but were about to get a bellyful of something much worse.

29

We had taken too long to counterattack. The spiders walked over the dying flares, blocking Dante's desperate gambit. The flares still had a few minutes in them but they were no longer strong enough to dissuade the spiders from having us for tea.

"Lasha, shoot them!" I cried.

Of course he chose this moment to be obstinate. "You say no shoot," he protested. The bloody things were a meter away from us now.

"I was wrong, okay? Shoot the ones over the torches. Dante, get ready."

Before I could cover my ears, Lasha had his Beretta 92 in his hands and was firing. He shot with laudable accuracy and although we faced ninety degrees of spiders approaching us, he quickly cleared up the space in front of us.

I handed Dante my water bottle and dug two more flares out of his bag. I lit them and tossed them as far back as I could. "Now," I said.

Dante held both liters in front of Lasha and asked him to shoot. The bullet went through and water came out like a faucet.

"Duck down," I said as the bottles went flying toward the flares.

We all had time to press our backs to the wall, get our bags in front of us and lower our heads so that our caving helmets faced the chamber. That took three seconds and if it had been any longer, I probably wouldn't be here to tell you about it.

You see, water reacts with magnesium to produce magnesium hydroxide and hydrogen gas. Hydrogen gas is, as you no doubt are aware, highly flammable and we instantly had a Hindenburg of an explosive fireball. It roared to life, flooding the chamber with light and heat and burned spiders. A wave of heat hit us but the fireball spread forward, burning dozens of giant spiders instantly. Remember, the Hindenburg was almost the length of the Titanic, and it burnt to nothing in thirty-four seconds.

For these mindless monsters, it was a world-ending inferno. Indeed, even though the chamber seemed massive, I worried about how much oxygen was being used up. The smell of burnt spiders was even worse than when they had been alive and I started to sweat. If our eyes hadn't adjusted to the brightness before, they certainly had now. The fire burned hot and fast, melting the giant spiders like they were marshmallows in a campfire. And then it too died. There were still some big spiders left, but our path forward was clear.

But, we were soon to find out, it did something else too. We rose to our feet, feeling jubilant at being alive but, at least for me, a little weirded out that I had just killed a thousand creatures or so.

"We have to move," Dante said.

"The only way back is forward," I said. I actually wouldn't have minded looking for a lever to that door. I didn't like being trapped in here. But what if I couldn't find it? Or there wasn't one? It was better to give myself hope, at least for now.

We moved forward, stepping on the hot stone floor covered in ash.

"That fireball really shouldn't have been that big," I said.

"Everything down here is wrong," Dante said.

"Well," I said. "Not everything. My singing was pretty great."

He gave me a dirty look. I was about to hum Waltzing Matilda just to annoy him when I heard it. The faint sound of leaves rustling. That wasn't right. Sand blowing in the wind? That wasn't right either, but something like that.

We reached the end of our straight line. To the left and to the right stretched identical chambers. Each was massive, like a wing in an airport. It was dark but it did look too symmetrical and too smooth to be natural.

"Which way?" I asked.

Dante held his hands up in an "I don't know and please don't ask me" kind of motion.

Lasha frowned and sniffed. He cocked his head slightly.

"What is sound?"

"That's a good question," I said. "I was wondering that too." The sound, whatever it was, was coming from the right. I looked as far as our torchlight would allow us.

I saw them coming for a long five seconds before my brain processed it. Spiders. Much smaller than the ones we'd just burned, but still bigger than a tarantula. And there were tens of thousands of them. Or more. Had the fire activated them? Were they babies of the bigger ones? I didn't know. All I knew was what I saw before me. An endless wave of arachnids swept across the chamber towards us.

"We go left!" I said, and we ran as fast as our heavy packs would allow.

Dante ran on my left and Lasha on my right. We had at least three meters on each side to the walls. Our feet slapped through ash and goo and spider gunk but we didn't (couldn't) care. The sound of the little spiders grew closer. Danta pulled his hammer out again.

"You can't fight them," I panted. Crikey, I wasn't in as good of shape as I used to be. This was a good reminder to keep going to the gym. "There's way too many."

He shrugged but saved his breath.

The sound of the horde behind us grew louder and then, horror of horrors, I felt one land on my neck.

Before I could react, Dante smashed it with the side of his hammer. My neck felt wet and sticky.

"Oi," I objected. I barely felt it though. There was too much going on to feel a little thing like a rock hammer striking the back of one's neck.

"It was about to bite. They could be venomous."

"Fair enough," I said. "Ta, mate." He stopped suddenly and I heard the hammer pounding into the ground. I would have gone back to help him (honest, I would) but my headlamp, turned up to maximum brightness, revealed our future.

Ahead of us was a deep, dark abyss that sank into the bowels of the earth. I'm not saying it was a bottomless pit, but for all intents and purposes it might as well have been. There was an ancient-looking wooden bridge that stretched across to the other side, some ten or twelve meters away.

"Lasha, get across that bridge," I said. "Be careful. That wood looks rotten."

He didn't slow. I turned and Dante almost ran into me. He was covered in gore and looked as disgusting as he was disgusted by the necessity of crushing spiders.

There was something bright green on his face. I wanted to ask but there was no time.

"Our way out," I said, pointing to the bridge behind us.

He nodded, though his eyes were only half open. I moved and he followed me, stumbling but staying on his feet. I glanced behind us. The ocean of spiders was at most four meters back. He had just killed some of the forerunners.

"We'll get across and knock the bridge down," I said. I know what you're thinking. I was thinking it, too. We would need that bridge to get back. But this was a one-step-at-a-time survival situation.

Lasha was halfway across. He went slowly and with good reason. Two of the planks had already crashed out of the bridge, tumbling away into the unknown. There was no rope to hang onto. Well, we had rope but no time to set it up. The sea of spiders was almost upon us. I could see their legs, tens of thousands of them, wriggling with urgent hunger.

"Go," Dante said. "I'm right behind you." He swayed as he spoke and I almost argued but there was no time and Dante was one of those guys who was easy-going until he got stubborn. And then he got really stubborn.

I gingerly stepped across the rotting wood. It was plenty wide, almost a meter, but the drop down went forever. It made me dizzy to think about. Twice the wood began to crumble beneath my feet. These planks had been down here, moldering in the darkness, for decades if not centuries. A light shone in my eyes and I realized Lasha had made it and was looking back at me.

It was bright enough that I almost stepped off into the darkness. I didn't even have time to say anything before the light dimmed and I heard him say, "Sorry."

The bridge shook. I glanced behind and saw Dante was on the bridge now. He was running, and leaking spiders like a dog shedding its winter coat. They flew in all directions, most of them into the void below us but a few onto the bridge.

"Slow down, mate," I said, slightly amused. He did not slow down and would soon barrel into me.

"Slow down," I said, much more urgently. I began to run even though I felt the bridge shaking from the force of my steps.

I was only five seconds from the other side when Dante bumped into me. I skidded off the bridge and just caught it with my right hand. He continued to run, almost not noticing me.

My backpack was heavy but I couldn't slip it off. I grabbed the board with my left hand too, so both of them were on the crumbling bridge as my body and feet dangled over the abyss.

I'm not going to lie. This was a low point for me. I began to scream and cry and beg for anyone to help me. I prayed to not just one god but as many as I could think of. When spiders began to crawl on my hands, I knew then there was no god. I would have to take care of it myself.

I couldn't see what happened to Dante so I tried to pull myself up. The pack was like an anchor that begged to drag me down. I let go with my left hand and slipped the strap off, then did the same thing with the right.

Fifty thousand dollars of equipment, not to mention my food and water, went tumbling into the abyss. But I was now unencumbered enough to pull myself up, slapping spiders away. Gaining my feet felt like I had won the lottery. I saw that Dante had reached the other side and fallen face first. That was a worry but as I took a step I suddenly had a much bigger worry. The much abused bridge collapsed under me. With a terrible finality, I fell into the chasm below.

30

That feeling of falling you sometimes get, the one that no scientists can explain and that wakes you up right before you fall asleep? I felt that exact feeling, about to enter the last, worst fall of my life, just when a rope appeared in my hands. Lasha, bless his heart, had been watching me. He had seen Dante push me off and taken immediate action. I grabbed onto that nylon like it was a miracle from above, which is exactly what it was.

Lasha grunted with effort as I cobbled my way up the rope. I could feel it sliding and that meant he was sliding. Where was Dante? With my pack on, we would have both tumbled below. As it was, my arms ached, but I pulled myself up. This was a second chance at life and I wasn't going to waste it. *Don't let go, don't let go, don't let go.*

I pulled myself up, gasping so hard I almost spewed but I finally reached the other side. Dante still lay face down where he had fallen coming off the bridge.

"Thank you," I said to Lasha, wrapping him in an embrace.

"I tell you I make it up for you," he said. "I owe you one more."

"Hey, we're even in my book, mate," I said, still hugging him hard. He looked offended.

I disengaged and took a look around. Everything looked different here on the far side. Instead of cold grey stone there was red sandstone and it felt warm. On the far side was an open doorway that led even deeper into this hell.

I had two unpleasant tasks to do so I did the slightly more pleasant one first. I glanced over at the far side. It was crawling with those baby spiders. Some were climbing down the steep side of the cliff but most had stopped.

"Haha, you bastards," I said but it was half-hearted at best. We were safely out of reach of the spiders. So then the second matter.

I had to check Dante, even though I think I already knew. With Lasha's help, I took off his backpack and turned him over. I was expecting something bad but I gasped and sank to my knees. He was as perforated as a fly swatter. His entire body was covered in bites that glowed with an unreal green. These spiders didn't have venom, they had some kind of nuclear waste! What the hell had the Soviets been doing down here?

The big man was already going cold and stiff. It felt like some nightmare I hadn't woken up from yet. I was disgusted at myself for bringing Nova and Dante into it. Why had that unpleasant person brought me the map? I felt no pulse so I pounded on his chest with wordless urgency.

"He dead," Lasha said sadly. "Too bad. Good man. Strong."

This seemed like faint praise and I wanted to berate him but then I remembered his friend had died recently and I hadn't even said as much as that.

"Lasha, we have to face the facts."

"What you mean?"

"Well we lost our water. Our flares. We can't get back across and even if we could and get past the spiders the door is locked. I lost my bag. My food." I thought about pushing Dante's body into the void. I thought about following him.

Lasha was practical as always. "You have new bag. Take. He not need."

I looked up at him but he had gone blurry.

"This whole thing was such a bloody mistake," I said. How had everything ended up so fully skew-whiff?

"So fix mistake," Lasha said.

It sounded so simple. I wanted to argue but his logic defeated my despair. I rose to my feet. I felt exhausted. But there was work to be done.

I put on Dante's pack and grunted. I had thought mine was heavy. This was thirty kilos easily.

"Help me, please," I said to Lasha. We grabbed Dante's body and dragged it into the open door. I wasn't going to leave him out here. I would remember him always. *Lest we forget.*

Inside was a sight the likes of which I had never seen before.

31

This room was round, made out of the same warm red sandstone as the platform outside. The air inside the ancient cave was thick with dampness and the scent of rock and the scent of long mouldering centuries. The walls were a tapestry of mineral veins, shimmering faintly in the dim light, their colors shifting between deep umbers, sickly greens, and spectral blues. Five plinths made out of the same stone rose from the ground, forming symmetrical pillars.

Pools of still water reflected the faint glow of bioluminescent fungi that clustered in the crevices, their eerie light casting shifting shadows across the cavern. In the silence, only the soft dripping of water echoed.

At the far end of the chamber, half-hidden behind a curtain of rocks, was a door formed from an alien material, so dark and smooth that it absorbed the light around it. The edges seemed fused with the surrounding rock, as if the cave itself grew around it. Faint, ancient symbols were etched into its surface.

We put Dante to rest against the back wall, slung off our packs, and walked slowly into the chamber.

"Don't touch anything," I said to Lasha, who nodded but his eyes were on the room. We looked around, did our due diligence, but soon I returned to the plinths. This part was, I knew in my bones, another necessary part.

Rule six of tomb raiding: there will always be something to play with. There were dials on the plinths showing various shapes in their own area. A small moveable arrow rested at the top in an empty space. Below them was writing, ancient writing, in a script I did not know, could not place. And believe me, I can place most scripts. It definitely wasn't the "spaghetti thrown at the wall" scripts of Georgia and Armenia but I asked Lasha anyway. He came over with his hands behind his back.

He peered at it with a show of concentration. "This I not know," he said. "But here. Look. Is Russian." He pointed to the bottom of the plinth. I somehow hadn't noticed. Someone had added translations by carving them into the plinth.

"Gordon Bennet," I said. "You bloody genius, Lasha."

"Is nothing," he said, but his cheeks flushed and he looked pleased.

"So let's have a look at these symbols, eh?"

There was one that looked like a smile with a straight line coming through it at a perpendicular angle. The next one was a spear or an arrow pointing to the right. The third puzzled me. Three hexes attached at angles, with three dots around them. One looked like a flame or leaf maybe. The next could have been a wave or a cloud. The last one was a star I guessed. The dial looked to be made of copper and was as green as it was any other color.

"What we do?" Lasha asked.

"We figure out the right symbol, using the script we found. When we do, something good will happen." *I hope.*

"What if we wrong?" Lasha asked.

I sighed and looked around. There was no sign of danger, no looming shadows or ominous soundtrack. But I knew the way these things worked.

"Let's just try to avoid that, eh?" I said. "Now let's have a look at what it says on this first one." I dropped to my knees and squinted. The writing was covered in dust but it wasn't hard to read.

"*No food I cook will ever fill me.*

And yet one simple drink will kill me," I read slowly.

"Easy," said Lasha.

"Yes it is," I agreed, wondering if it was *too* easy. There was only one thing that was used to cook but could not survive getting wet. A sense of dread filled me. I looked above to see if there were spikes or a hidden chamber. Then I checked below me as well. It seemed safe. "Well, here we go," I sighed. I pulled my hand into my sleeve and turned the copper dial to the shape that looked like a leaf or flame. Even through the cloth of my shirt, it was cold.

Nothing happened. Well that might not be so bad. We were still alive, and it was with that gratitude that we moved to the second plinth. It had the same copper dial with the same symbols. We translated the words at the bottom together.

"Feathered, I fly

Landing, I die

What strange bird am I?"

We looked at the symbols. Not the smile. Spear. Probably not the three hexes. We had already used the flame. Wave? Cloud? Star?

"This one," Lasha said. He pointed at the spear and made a show of drawing back an arrow.

"Bow and arrow. Yes, arrows!"

I turned the dial to the arrow. Again nothing happened. In my excitement, I was convinced that was a sign we were doing well.

"Alright, we're halfway done," I said to Lasha. "After this we can take a break. Eat something." The truth is I didn't want to stop. I didn't want to have time to think. I needed to move forward and get lost with action and doing. But I also knew the merits of keeping up morale.

We moved to the third plinth. We were now more than halfway into the chamber. I glanced over at the eerie door. Was this puzzle going to reveal a key? I hoped so. Otherwise we might have to try to bash our way in, and I found that usually people who prepare chambers such as these account for the brute force factor rather thoroughly.

The same dial was on the third plinth, also resting in a neutral position. We translated the Russian, though I wondered again at the original language.

I'm hung by my crown;
Fleets stop when I drown.

Well that one was pretty easy. What entered water and stopped a ship? Besides, we had a love affair with anchors in Australia. I had seen the Sirius Anchor in Sydney just a few months ago.

"Ah," I said, suddenly realizing. "The smile with a line. It's an anchor."

"Yes, not smile," Lasha said. "No think smile."

"No worries," I said, although it was funny that I had made such a cultural blunder. I was so used to smilies and smile emojis I hadn't even thought about any other options. The dour man had not made the same mistake.

I moved the third arrow, just one spot down. Again nothing happened. A perverse part of me wanted to move it to the wrong one just to see. That could be an expensive experiment though.

"Righto, mate," I said. "Let's finish this fourth one and see what we can see." We moved over the fourth plinth. Now the dark door was not far away at all. I felt it there, pulsating with existence.

This was the longest one by far and it took us a little while to come up with the translation.

A thousand soldiers guard this golden hoard,
Each with a single sword;
Only one door, and entrance is abhorred
But golden riches is the reward

I ran through the various symbols. We had used the smile, the spear, and the flame. That left the three hexes, the wave, the cloud, and the star. Of course I was here for treasure. The map had led me here. But which of those symbols indicated treasure?

There was a sound from back by the chasm, as of leaves rustling. A forest of leaves moving in a stiff, hairy breeze. A terrible feeling dawned in my heart and instantly sunk down to my stomach.

"Lasha," I said. "Would you mind having a look out by that big bloody hole we crossed?"

I stared at the dial as he hurried out. I was thinking about using the cloud. It symbolized growth and cycles and life. That was close to treasure. In my mind's eye, I saw Nova shake her head at me in a "you know better than that" motion.

"It isn't the bloody cloud," I muttered.

Lasha returned quickly, out of breath.

"Spiders," he said. "Many spiders. They come over hole."

"Well, stink," I said with a sigh.

32

It was starting to feel not fair, like someone was picking on us. It was just one thing after another. I'm in general a chilled out guy but this was beginning to test me.

"How long do we have?"

He looked unhappy. "Less than minute."

I looked over the room. There was no door there, nothing we could close. We had used most of our flares, and only had two left for absolute emergencies. Oh well.

"Lasha, burn your flares. Put them in the doorway."

"Nothing left? For emergency," he said. Every caver fears getting stuck in the dark, so I understood his worry. But we had bigger problems at the moment.

"We've got backup batteries. We don't have backup lives!" I snapped.

He considered that and then crossed to his pack. He moved quickly but by the time he got the flare out, the first spider appeared in the doorway. I kicked it, and it sailed like a rugby ball to land four meters away with a satisfying splat. But there were more, so many more, crawling up out of the chasm.

Lasha dropped the flares and the room went bright red. The hissing of the flares and it smelled like the kind of sparkler you would use at a children's birthday party. The spiders paused and the ones in front tried to push their way back. I thought about using our last water bottle for a bomb, but I didn't want to risk the fireball coming our way and damaging the plinths or ourselves.

We grabbed our bags and ran back to the last plinth. I read the puzzle again.

A thousand soldiers guard this golden hoard,
Each with a single sword;
Only one door, and entrance is abhorred
But golden riches is the reward

"Any idea what that means?" I asked Lasha.

He nodded and said, "Golden hoard. It means treasure."

I stared at him and then smiled. "Okay thanks." That wasn't helpful but then I wondered. Could it actually be that simple? The fire still burned bright but it illuminated the cavern beyond. Most of the small spiders had reached this side, it seemed. I looked at the three hexes, the wave, the cloud, and the star.

I must have misidentified one of them. The star could be a raindrop maybe. Or a gleam. That was treasure related. The cloud had to be a cloud. The wave or leaf? And what were these three hexes? What could they be? I needed to know that most of all.

I almost had it then, but the sound of gunfire broke my attention. A few spiders were being pushed from behind into and over our flares. Lasha made sure they did not get far. The gunfire echoed in the cavern and I winced.

My mind was a blank. Look, if you've figured this out, feel free to be smug right now. But I tell you, it's much harder to think under pressure than it is while you're sitting there with your eyes on a page. And you can't get much more pressure than this. *Treasure.*

The firing stopped.

"Out of ammo," Lasha said. "Fire not keep them out for much longer." The spiders were pressing forward. The flares scorched some of them, but many others were going over them. They would be in the chamber in seconds.

I looked back at my plinth. Better to take a guess and risk whatever damage it might or might not do. *A single sword.* Why specify that? And then, belatedly, it hit me.

A thousand soldiers, with a single sword. Guarding golden treasure.

"Lasha," I cried in delight. "It's bees!"

"Bees?" he asked. "It be what?" He was busy kicking and stomping the spiders, creating pools of glowing green goo.

I didn't answer him. I instead turned the copper dial to the three hexes, which I now realized was a honeycomb. The three little dots around them were so obviously bees now.

I turned the dial just as dozens of spiders spilled into the room, all around Lasha. There was no sound, no clicking or rumbling. But as I looked over, I saw that the strange black door had opened.

"Lasha, get inside." He ran back to me and scooped up his backpack.

"Take mine too," I asked. Well, requested firmly.

He looked at me in surprise. "You not come?"

"Go. I'll be right there."

Behind him, the large door began to close, as silently as it had opened.

"Go!" I said. He clearly wanted to ask more but there was no time. There were probably fifty spiders in the room now and the torches were buried under the dead flesh of their comrades. Soon there would be thousands. I ran to the entrance, stomping them with fury. One crawled up my leg and I punched it so hard it splattered on my fist and my leg. There were then too many to smash and I had to let them crawl up me. One was on Dante's chest and I squashed it with my boot.

"Okay, big man," I said. "Get ready." Dante weighed one hundred kilograms at a bare minimum. I heaved him onto my back, dislodging several more spiders. Thinking about it now, I must have been full of adrenaline, like the mums who lift a car to save their children. At the time, I just felt a desperate need to prevent my friend from becoming spider food. I turned and stumbled through the chamber.

The big dark door was closing slowly but it was halfway closed now. Dante was slipping off my shoulders and I had to pause to readjust. I could just see in my torchlight Lasha's face in the darkness.

"Come, hurry."

I ran as fast as I've ever run, but I could see it wasn't going to work. The door was mostly closed now.

"Duck," I shouted. I did not wait to see if he listened. I turned my body sideways and launched Dante into the gap. His body rubbed against one wall and fell but most of his body was on the inside. I was still perpendicular to the door, and I leapt in using all my momentum.

I half-landed on Dante's body. His foot stuck out the door and a spider crawled on it. The door pressed against his ankle. Lasha grabbed his arms and pulled him in, scraping off the spider.

We were all inside just as the door slid closed and left us in the darkness.

33

Rule nine of tomb raiding: there will always be different paths. This is what waited for us as I turned up my headlamp. Three paths leading deeper into the caves. Each was a similar looking tunnel. One led to the right, one to the left and one was in the center.

I sat on the floor for a few minutes, catching my breath and recovering from the mad run that had just got me into the room. Finally I realized that Lasha was looking right at me.

"Why you bring him?" Lasha asked. He pointed at Dante's body, slumped on a wall about a meter away from us.

The question surprised me. I thought about it for a moment. "Oh mate. I don't know. It just didn't feel right, leaving him there to be spider chow."

"You almost die," he said.

I shrugged. "It looks like we all will die down here, sooner rather than later."

He frowned. "Later better. We need work together. Two may live, one will die. No be stupid."

I belatedly realized his issue. He thought I had risked him and his survival. Come to think of it, he was right. "Lasha, mate, I'm sorry. I should have thought about you. I just panicked. Dante has been my right-hand man for a long time. He's been … a friend. I think I found it hard to say goodbye."

"Now is time for live. Later, time for friend."

"Okay, let's live," I agreed. I rose to my feet and sighed. "So which way do you want to go? The long dark corridor that leads to certain death, the long dark corridor that leads to certain death, or, to really switch things up, the long dark corridor that leads to certain death?"

"It not matter."

"Right. Well let's go down the middle then."

We left our big packs behind and walked for a few hours. The walls were clean and warm with no side passages that I could see. I might have checked, if my equipment hadn't fallen down a pit but then I might not have. I was having a difficult time trying to care about anything. We should have quit after an hour but I felt like we had already gone so far. After two, we had definitely gone too far to turn back. But after three hours, with nothing changing, we turned around, pausing only to mark our destination with chalk on the right wall. It was a hard walk back. Our headlamps were going dim when we finally got back to the chamber with Dante's body.

"I picked poorly, so you can choose next," I said. He looked at the passages and pointed at the left one.

"Any particular reason?" I asked.

"Just guess."

"That's as good a reason as any."

This time we only went two hours in before turning around. We argued for a bit about going for longer but the same featureless walls and lack of adjoining rooms discouraged us. We marked the spot we had gotten to here as well and turned around.

By the time we got back, we were in complete darkness. We searched both our bags and only found enough batteries for one headlamp. I insisted Lasha take it: I could follow behind him and use his torchlight.

"Grab everything you can," I said grimly. "We're not coming back this time."

We took everything out of the bags except for food and what little water we had left. The scuba gear, electronic instruments, waterproof clothes, and so on we just left behind in a chaotic jumble of a pile. As it grew, I began to think of it as a kind of burial treasure for Dante.

Finally our bags were light enough. I knelt beside Dante's stiff body and tried to think of something to say.

"Cheers, mate," was all I could summon up. As far as last words go, they left something to be desired. I knew that, but I had lost so much, including my power of always knowing the right thing to say.

I rose to my feet and we began the final leg. I was mentally prepared for a death march. I pictured our skeletons, lying in some far flung end of the tunnel. Thus I started laughing when, less than ten minutes into our journey, Lasha's light shone upon a reinforced, keypad-locked door with the keypad smashed open. Inside was a room stuffed with otherworldly treasure.

34

I grabbed Lasha by the shoulders and looked him in the eyes, squinting a little from the bright headlamp on his head. I was enormously excited but also well aware of the smashed door panel. There was no telling when that had happened. I raised my finger to my lips and indicated we should move in cautiously.

That caution lasted about three seconds, lost as soon as we stepped into the room. It was enormous, as big as the inside of Flinders Station (say, some two city blocks) and lit up by some kind of electronic torches. Inside lay a mix of treasures: gold artifacts, ancient scrolls, strange modern equipment, humanoid figures frozen in glass cylinders, a clock ticking backward with no apparent power source, a map etched into a sheet of unmelting ice, an ornate crown that whispered in an unknown language, a stack of books, a sword hovering inches above the ground as if repelled by gravity, and piles of coins stacked waist high in places.

There was not anyone else in the room. I'm afraid we quite lost our minds. Friends, you wouldn't believe some of the things I discovered in that chamber. But I will tell you about some of the more believable discoveries we made, especially in what we assumed was in the Soviet corner. There was Nochnoy Ogon, a hellish, self-aware firebomb. Lasha discovered the Koschei Protocol, an immortality serum once used to create Soviet super-soldiers. This serum would strip soldiers of their humanity, binding their souls to a state-issued Red Star badge. As long as the object remained intact, they would be unkillable, fighting on even after their bodies had rotted. There was an enormous warhead with a name that translated to something like "Gorgon's Gaze." The missile had a picture of Medusa on it and according to the documentation, instead of a traditional explosion, it would unleash a pulse that froze all living beings within its blast radius into grotesque statues. There was much more than that, but you have some idea of the bloody insane world we had entered.

Then there were the guns that Lasha and I looked at for several breathless moments. If the documentation, a typed up paper protected by lamination, could be believed, these weapons had been created by the Soviets and imbued with incredible powers. The AKM-Заговор (AKM-Zagovor, "Enchantment") claimed to have self-replenishing ammunition, curse-infused rounds, something called a witchfire bayonet, eldritch durability, and a mode called "whisper or wail."

This fascinated me. Not because I believed any of it, but because it was proof that the even skeptical Soviets were capable of falling for esoteric nonsense. Just like the Nazis, some foolish old general had swallowed his credulity and fallen for the idea of magical weapons. Or, more likely, some higher up had demanded it and a clever underling had mocked up some cunning prototype. But one thing above all others caught my eye.

It was an ancient book with a flame on the cover. I don't mean an illustration or carving of a flame. There was a small fire on the book cover. It was warm to the touch but burned neither my hands nor the book itself. I heard a voice whisper in my head: *the Promethean fire*.

I opened the book with wide eyes. It was written in a kind of cuneiform known as Ugaritic. This I knew well, as I had studied it in the United States at the University of Wisconsin. I read quietly out loud while Lasha ran around the chamber, stuffing his backpack with treasures. The book swallowed my attention so completely I forgot where I was.

35

Author's Note:

For those who aren't conversant in Greek myth, the following is pretty shocking information. It doesn't match up with other extant historical mythological accounts. Prometheus isn't connected with the Golden Fleece. Is it useful to talk about the veracity of myths and legends? Maybe, maybe not. I'm starting to wonder about where to draw the line between folk tales and history, anyway.

The Argo cut through the waves, a living thing of wood and will, its mast creaking under the weight of destiny. Jason stood at the prow, eyes fixed on the mist-shrouded shores of Colchis. He had journeyed far with those heroes of renown that history would dub the Argonauts. They had fought many battles; overcome untold hardships. Yet all their might and courage would be for nothing without one woman.

Medea, high priestess of Hecate, stood beside him. Her dark eyes were pools of knowledge deeper than the sea itself. It was she who had whispered the Fleece's true nature to Jason when first they met in secret. More than a symbol of kingship, the Golden Fleece was a thing of power: a pelt from a divine ram that could heal any wound, cure any disease, even return the dead to life.

It all went back to Prometheus. His Titan blood had spilled into the earth and from it, fennel and oregano had sprung. After Prometheus was freed, those plants had been eaten by a lone, wandering sheep. The ram was infused with titanic power that lasted long after its own death.

That power had kept Medea's father strong, his warriors unmatched. Had given them undying warriors who eventually became grim skeletons. Jason's quest was no longer simply one of honor or inheritance. It was a challenge to death itself.

King Aeëtes did not give willingly. He had scowled upon his golden throne when Jason, standing proud before him, demanded the Fleece. The king, like the dragon who coiled around the sacred tree that held the pelt, would protect his treasure with his life.

"The Fleece is no mere prize for an upstart boy," Aeëtes said. "If you seek it, you must prove your worth." He set Jason three trials: to yoke the fire-breathing bulls of Ares, to sow the dragon's teeth, and to defeat the warriors that would spring from them. He thus intended to slay Jason, but without fear of reprisal from his crew of brave men or distant King Pelias.

Jason, fearless yet uncertain, turned to Medea. That night, she met him under the full moon, the scent of crushed herbs thick in the air around her. She traced sigils of power on his skin; whispered spells into his ear. With each syllable, his limbs grew stronger, his mind sharper. Finally, she gave him a vial of enchanted oil to coat his body against flame.

With her magic infusing his body and soul, he defeated the bulls, though their breath was hot enough to char bone. With her wisdom, he scattered the dragon's teeth across the black earth. When the warriors clawed their way into the world, Medea whispered, "Throw a stone among them."

Jason obeyed. The undying men turned upon each other in confusion, slaying themselves before they could strike him. The Argonauts cheered, but Jason knew victory was far from his grasp.

Aeëtes plotted Jason's death directly. What other choice had he? The Fleece belonged to him and his people and the proud ruler could not allow it to be stolen. Medea, knowing her father's heart, acted first. In the dead of night, she guided Jason through the palace, down hidden corridors until they reached the sacred grove.

The Fleece hung from the oak: its golden wool shimmering in the moonlight; its magic pulsing like a heartbeat. A serpent, enormous as a river, coiled around the tree. Medea stepped forward. From her lips poured ancient honeyed words, a lullaby of power and sleep. The serpent swayed, hissed once, then fell still.

Jason seized the Fleece in his calloused hands. At once, warmth coursed through his limbs, filling him with a strength unlike anything he had known. All his aches and pains and bruises were gone in the blinking of an eye. He turned to Medea, wonder in his eyes.

"We must go," she said, voice tight with urgency.

They fled to the Argo, their path stained with betrayal and blood. Medea's own kin pursued them, her brother Apsyrtus among them. She knew her father's wrath, knew he would never stop until the Fleece was returned: not until he had her heart on a pike. They set sail but never could they elude their pursuers.

On the open sea, Aeëtes's ships closed in. Jason gripped the Fleece as if its power alone could save them. But Medea knew better. When the cold light of dawn showed that her brother Apsyrtus had nearly caught them, her decision was made.

She whispered to Jason, voice heavy with sorrow. "There is only one way for us to escape. The price of our future must be paid by severing the past."

She called Apsyrtus to her under a banner of false peace. When he came, trusting, she struck. Her knife entered his heart and his blood blackened the waves. Taking Jason's sword, she cut her brother into pieces and cast his limbs into the sea. This would, she knew, force her father to stop and collect them, giving the Argo time to flee.

Jason did not meet her eyes for many days.

They returned to Iolcus triumphant, the Fleece glittering in Jason's hands. But his uncle, King Pelias, who had usurped Jason's throne, scoffed.

"You expect me to yield simply because you bring back a sheep's skin?" he sneered.

Jason's hand tightened around the pelt. "This is no mere skin. It holds the power to heal, to grant life."

Pelias laughed. "Prove it."

Medea stepped forward, her gaze cold as a winter sea. "Give me a ram."

A servant brought a frail creature, its wool patchy, its legs shaking. Medea took Jason's blade and, without hesitation, cut its throat. Pelias smirked.

Medea draped the Fleece over the carcass and whispered in the language of gods. The air thickened, pulsed. The golden wool shimmered, then blazed with light. The ram shuddered. Its limbs twitched. Then, impossibly, it stood: whole, its fleece brighter than before. While an ancient beast had been led into the room and slaughtered, now only an animal in prime strength and vitality remained.

The hall fell silent.

Pelias's daughters, trembling, fell to their knees. "Our father is old," they pleaded. "Will you not grant him youth?"

Medea turned to Jason, and he nodded. With feigned solemnity, she instructed the princesses. They, desperate for their father's rebirth, took up their knives. Pelias did not have time to protest before he was cut down by his daughters.

The king's blood ran fast. The Fleece shimmered, but Medea's voice did not rise in song. Pelias's body lay still, his soul beyond the reach of the gods. The daughters wailed and cried but they were fatherless and were soon led to the dungeons for the crimes of regicide and patricide.

Jason took his throne, but victory rang hollow. The Fleece, for all its power, could not restore what was lost: his love for Medea. She, though his savior, became a fearful villain to him.

Eventually, many years later, he betrayed her for another. Medea once again did not hesitate. She was not one to let attachments from the past affect the decisions of her present. And so she took from him the most precious things he had: his sons. She also took the Fleece and returned, legends say, to Colchis. Here she was not welcome and so she left the Fleece and wandered until she came to the land of the Medes. She lived long there and was lost from history.

Jason was alone, bereft of family, of wife, and of treasure. Is it any wonder he also gave up the Kingship? He wandered to the Argo, where he had once stood a hero. The ship, long rotted, bore his weight one final time before the mast cracked, falling upon him, ending his tale.

36

I closed the book as my eyes sought Lasha. He had an Enchantment rifle cradled in his arms and a big smile on his face. He walked over to me.

"This good gun," he said when he saw my attention.

"Mmm-hmm," I said. I wasn't really listening. "Hey, Lasha, have you seen anything that looks like a sheepskin?"

He nodded. "Yes. Right there," he said. He pointed at an alcove I had not noticed.

Within was a pile of swords and shields stacked up. On the top of a two meter high stack of shields, resting almost casually, lay a golden sheepskin. It sparkled in the air with a vibrant energy and there was an aura around it like a golden and silver version of the Northern Lights.

My jaw dropped. It all made sense, in a nonsensical way. The assassins along the way. The resistance from the minute I had received the map. The deadly opposition willing to do anything to stop us. It had all been for this. *The Golden Fleece.*

I don't know why I believed in this. Maybe it was simply because I needed it to be real. For all my skepticism, I was a rube when my emotions got involved. Just like every other chump out there.

"Is there an exit?" I asked Lasha. "Take a look."

"We leave?" he asked.

"Not yet," I said.

I took the Fleece in my hand. For all the energy swirling around it, the thing felt surprisingly mundane. Heavy, though. Much heavier than I expected. I clutched it in both my hands and jogged out of the treasure chamber and back down the hall.

One phrase resonated in my head: *Medea draped the Fleece over the carcass and whispered in the language of gods.*

I know it took five minutes or more to get back to the crossroads, but I don't remember a second of it. I just remember stumbling out into the chamber, seeing Dante's body slumped on the floor, and kneeling beside him.

What was I doing? He was dead, deader than dead. He had been punctured by a thousand spider bites, leaving him filled with radioactive venom. Reality came crashing down on me and I almost walked away. But what did I have to lose?

I moved Dante to his back and lay him with his arms by his side. He was already going stiff but I managed. Then I covered him with the Fleece. Dante was a big man but he was pretty much completely covered by it. What next? I put the book in my large coat pocket.

Medea draped the Fleece over the carcass and whispered in the language of gods.

I knew a lot of languages but not the language of the gods. I wondered what language Medea might have spoken in, if the source could be trusted. Maybe it didn't matter. The book had said that Medea served the goddess Hecate, so I addressed her, using the tune of an old fast food jingle.

Hecate Hecate

Be lucky, Unsicken, and undo the cut.

Feeling it wouldn't hurt, and since I was already on my knees, I prostrated myself to the warm ground. I closed my eyes and concentrated on my need and my willpower. Though my voice was muffled, I sang again my holy request. To acknowledge the sacred moment, I put my hand on my heart. I could feel the map just below my jacket and was somehow surprised it was still there.

Hecate Hecate

Be lucky, Unsicken, and undo the cut.

With a long sigh, I stood up. Dante's eyes met mine.

"Blimey, I've got a headache," he said. "And why am I under this bloody wool blanket?"

I surprised both of us by wrapping him in the biggest hug I've ever given. After a few seconds, he pulled back.

"Alright, alright. What happened? Last thing I remember is running across that bridge."

I paused as I considered what to say. How to tell him. How much to tell him.

"I passed out, eh?" he said. "Where's Lasha?"

Better to rip the plaster off entirely, I decided.

"You died, mate," I said.

"I feel like it," he said. "Can't remember a thing."

"No. You feel like it because you died. For hours. Spider bites were too much."

"I don't really know what this bit is. I don't find it funny," he said. He actually sounded really annoyed.

"It's not a bit. God's honest truth. I swear to you on Nova's memory it happened."

"How dare you bring up her name? You tasteless arsehole!" Dante never swore. It was one of his few weaknesses. The fact that he did so here and now revealed his agitated state of mind.

"Look at the bloody sheepskin on you, mate! We didn't have that before." I stopped because I realized invoking the existence of the legendary Golden Fleece might not help my argument.

Dante glanced at the door we had just gotten through and changed the subject. "So we're on the inside now?"

"Yeah and there are about a million spiders outside just waiting for us."

He smiled at that. "Rule seven of tomb raiding: there's always something to be killed."

"Hey don't quote me to me. I get to say the rules."

"Who says?"

"I do. I make the rules!"

He stood slowly, gingerly. The Golden Fleece fell to the floor. I almost did too, out of sheer, unbridled shock. He looked good. There wasn't any sign of the bites on him. No bruises, no wounds at all.

"So what's the play?" he asked.

I had to try one more time. I reached out and put my hand on his shoulder.

"I know it's a lot," I said. "But you have to believe me. You died and came back to life. It's a miracle, a biblical moment in history. It's stunning. You have returned from the darkness. You are reborn. Christ, you don't have a scratch on you, you lucky unpleasant person."

He made a sound of inarticulate frustration, but whatever he was going to say was lost as we were interrupted.

"What? You alive?" Lasha leaned his Enchantment rifle against the wall and ran out from the tunnel and stared up at Dante like he was a zoo exhibition.

"You see, I was right to protect him," I said. No one likes an I-told-you-so, but I think it's important to trust your instincts.

"Really?" Lasha said. He stretched out and touched Dante on the arm. When he felt solid flesh, he flinched away, as though he had expected a hologram or a ghost.

"Jad put you up to this?" Dante asked Lasha. But I heard uncertainty in his voice. We fell into a brief silence that was soon filled by an unexpected source.

"They're in there!" a muffled voice from the outer chamber.

"Get the door open," said another. "And *something something* these spiders!" It was a little hard to hear, but there was no doubt about the tone. Someone was giving orders. And they were coming for us.

37

Hi there! It's me, the nephew. Now this is the part of the story I was dreading to include because, well, yeah, it's just a little hard to believe. I myself certainly wondered what kind of fiction that Uncle Jad was writing when I first read this. Was he just exaggerating to make a good story better? Had he been deceived or become delusional? I considered about a million different possibilities. The one thing I didn't really think about was if he was telling the truth.

In the intervening months, however, I did some research. I'll tell you a little about what I found and then show you a conversation I had with Dr. Elene Nefaridze at the University of Georgia. (I include that here with her permission, of course.) Then we'll get back to the story as soon as possible.

I read a lot of classics and in Ovid's *Metamorphoses* I found the following quote, in a prayer that asks for the aid of the goddess Hecate.

'Night, most faithful keeper of our secret rites;
Stars, that, with the golden moon, succeed the fires of light;
Triple Hecate, you who know all our undertakings,
and come, to aid the witches' art, and all our incantations:
You, Earth, who yield the sorceress herbs of magic force:
You, airs and breezes, pools and hills, and every watercourse;
Be here; all you Gods of Night, and Gods of Groves endorse.
Streams, at will, by banks amazed, turn backwards to their source.
I calm rough seas, and stir the calm by my magic spells:
bring clouds, disperse the clouds, raise storms and storms dispel;
and, with my incantations, I break the serpent's teeth;

So what does all that mean? The truth is that I still don't know, although some of those phrases make me feel uncomfortable. They have stuck in my head, like the terrible flip side of a pop song that gets stuck in your head. An ear serpent rather than an ear worm, if you will. Anyway, I got lost in reading and so sent some emails to an expert. Here is how our conversation went.

Subject: Inquiry About the Legend of the Golden Fleece

Dear Professor Nefaridze,

I hope this email finds you well. I am a recent university graduate researching myths and legends. I am particularly interested in the legend of the Golden Fleece and its connections to ancient Colchis. I understand that Georgia has a rich historical and archaeological perspective on this legend, and I was hoping you could provide some insights.

I am curious about whether the Golden Fleece is purely a myth or if there are historical elements that could have inspired it. I have read theories suggesting that the Fleece could be linked to ancient gold panning techniques in the rivers of Colchis. Do you think there is any archaeological evidence to support this? What is the link to the goddess Hecate?

I would greatly appreciate any information or resources you could share. Thank you for your time.

Subject: Re: Inquiry About the Legend of the Golden Fleece

Thank you for your email and for your interest in the legend of the Golden Fleece. It is indeed a fascinating topic with deep roots in Georgian history and culture. While the myth itself originates from Greek mythology (specifically the tale of Jason and the Argonauts,) there are strong indications that it was inspired by real historical practices in ancient Colchis (modern-day western Georgia).

The theory you mentioned about gold panning is one of the most widely accepted explanations. Ancient Colchians are believed to have used sheepskins to trap gold particles from mountain rivers, a technique that was documented by historians such as Strabo. Some archaeological findings, including remnants of gold-mining sites, support the idea that Colchis was renowned for its wealth and advanced metallurgy.

Culturally, the Golden Fleece remains a powerful symbol in Georgia. You will find references to it in Georgian literature, art, and even in the national narrative of resilience and prosperity. We hold that the Fleece had medical knowledge on it, that it was in essence the first book of medicine. In fact, the English word "medicine" is derived from Medea, the keeper of the Fleece.

The connection with Hecate would likely have come through Medea, who was known by some as "The Shadow Queen." But this is not an accidental one. Hecate is, according to some sources, the real mother of Medea. This was probably just a phrase to indicate Medea's power and witchy status, since Circe at times was described the same way. Regardless, Medea is the goddess of witches, enchantments, and charms. Wanderers, sages and herb collectors alike would pray to Hecate at full moon, usually at a crossroads. She was also known as or associated with Luna the moon goddess, Proserpina, and Diana, and she is maybe the only known goddess to have a dog as one of her animals. According to Hesiod, she was "the one who Zeus respects above all." The important thing is that she was a liminal figure, a Goddess of Boundaries, whether she upholds them, or crosses them. The ultimate boundary, of course, is that between life and death, which links her to the medicinal properties of the Fleece.

If you would like to explore this further, I recommend looking into the work of Georgian historian Otar Lordkipanidze, who has written extensively on the subject. I would also be happy to answer any specific questions you may have.

Best regards,
Dr. Elene Nefaridze

Subject: Re: Re: Inquiry About the Legend of the Golden Fleece
Dr. Nefaridze,

Thank you so much for your reply. It has helped me immensely in my attempt to understand this issue further. I simply have one further question. I also came across references to Prometheus being bound in the Caucasus Mountains, which are in the same region as Colchis. Is there any connection between his myth and the legend of the Golden Fleece?

Subject: Re: Re: Re: Inquiry About the Legend of the Golden Fleece

Regarding Prometheus, you are correct that his myth is also linked to the Caucasus Mountains. According to Greek mythology, Zeus punished Prometheus by chaining him to a mountain in this region as an eternal torment for giving fire to humanity. This suggests that the Greeks viewed the Caucasus as a place of both suffering and mystique. Some scholars believe that this duality, both punishment (Prometheus) and wealth (the Golden Fleece), contributed to Colchis's portrayal as a land of both danger and opportunity. In addition, both Hecate and Prometheus were Titans who sided with Zeus in the war against their own kind, so they could have had a relationship or at least have a similar use as a motif. I hope that helps!

Best regards,
Dr. Elene Nefaridze

That answered some questions for me. Hopefully it does for you too! Back to Uncle Jad's story!

38

We looked at each other in horror and suspense as the voices came closer. It hadn't taken me that long to solve the riddle of the door, and for all that I knew they already knew the answers to the riddles. This was not a good place to be in.

"Lasha," I said, speaking slowly and quietly. "Did you see any exit in the treasure chamber room?"

He shook his head. "This I not find."

That settled it. "Grab your gun. Dante, are you able to pick up the Fleece?"

Dante almost looked offended at the suggestion that he might have trouble. In silent answer, he hefted the skin onto his shoulders. Lasha paced back and scooped up the gun. We didn't even know if it would work, but it was the only defense we had.

"We can't go back into the treasure room," I said. "We'll be pinned in and trapped." I felt confident this was true but the profound sense of loss that only getting that cursory glance at the ultimate treasure trove hurt me deeply. All we had was the book in my hands, the Enchantment rifle, the Golden Fleece, and whatever was in Lasha's pack. Well, that perhaps wasn't such a bad haul after all, I mused. We stood in the middle tunnel, the first one that we had explored.

The door opened suddenly. The air around us froze with tension. When several men dressed in rustic woolen vests and sheepskin caps entered, I realized I had somehow known all along it would be them.

The Shepherds.

There were a dozen of them, at least. They all had lean bodies, prominent beards and homespun clothes. Most of them had Uzis in hand but at least one of them, near the back, appeared to be holding a flamethrower. They saw us moments after we had clocked them. One of them called back a warning. There were no spiders to be seen but a horrible roasted smell came through the door.

Lasha said something in Georgian, something he would later tell me translated to something unprintable. He raised the gun. For something that was fifty plus years old, it looked sleek. There were a few modes and nozzles that made it look like a squirt gun, but overall it did look deadly.

That was all the time I had to see because Lasha opened fire. The gun was, in a word, crazy. The bullets it fired sounded like mortar fire but I could see them, twisting in the air and hunting down the men in the doorway. Four of them dropped to the ground in as many seconds and the others scattered.

Lasha said, panting, "I no afraid anymore."

Idiot that I was, I was feeling good. We had scattered the enemies and bought ourselves time. Perhaps we could even advance on them and escape back the way we had come. That was when the grenade bounced in. It was big and made a tinking sound as it came to a rest a few meters into the room.

"Get back!" I yelled. This was unnecessary, as my companions also had both eyes and legs. We all ran as far down the tunnel as we could. Less than ten seconds later, the boom hit. I don't know what kind of force was in that thing, but the shockwaves knocked Lasha and I to the ground. Dante kept his feet but had to do a little dance in order to do so.

"What's at the end of this tunnel?" Dante asked.

I shrugged. "We went down for a few hours and saw nothing."

"Let's go back and fight," Lasha said. I didn't know if he had permanently acquired this new state of bravery or perhaps he was just buoyed by the possession of an awesome weapon. Perhaps there was no difference.

The sound of cracking rock came from the tunnel behind us. "I'm not sure we want to go back," I said. A cave-in was worse than death.

The sound of voices drew closer.

"We should get going," Dante said. The air was cold but he had the light sheen of a sweat. I turned my headlamp torch on high. I saw the shapes, shadows really, of three men advancing through the distant darkness. All of them had guns and though I couldn't see what the guns were exactly, they were bigger than Uzis. An uneasy feeling stirred in my gut. Could there have been enough time?

"Lasha, put your gun on curse mode and fire!" I said. Vaguely I remembered having some compunction about taking human life, but that had been a lifetime ago. Lasha muttered and fiddled with his gun.

"Kill the light, mate," Dante said urgently.

He dropped down to one knee and I switched off my headlight and followed him. Just in time. Bullets screamed over our heads. And that's not a figure of speech. They screamed like banshees as they tore through the air and some part of my reptilian brain knew that if they hit me, I was dead. Lasha fired back: his bullets made a different sound but an equally ominous one.

"Run," I said. We tore through the tunnel. We knew we could go quickly at least until we reached the place I had marked on our first trip down the tunnel. Though Lasha and I lagged, Dante was a running machine. He was one of those weirdos who ran marathons and ultra marathons for fun, but I was relieved that he was moving so well.

He had been dead. The mind boggled at the limits of the Fleece. Would it work on a skeleton? On ashes? Did it have to be a recent death? Did the prayer to Hecate do anything? If you wore it as a cape, would you be invulnerable to harm?

These were my thoughts as we fled for hours down the tunnel. There's a point where you get tired but then there's a point where tiredness doesn't matter and you can just walk forever. Yes, there's a death march quality to this, but we were aware of pursuers and only stopped to rest for fifteen or twenty minutes at a time. We had no food, no water (even our last pack had been left behind). We kept going and going and by my watch we traveled for just under fourteen hours, heading ever up, before we saw sunlight ahead of us.

We emerged cautiously to a windswept bluff. Yellow flowers grew in bunches amidst bunches of wild grass. Below us was a small lake and when Lasha saw it, his face went through a series of contortions. He started shaking his head in denial.

"No, no, no," he said.

I looked at Dante, who returned a puzzled look my way. So I grabbed Lasha's arm and asked him a gentle question.

"What the fuck is wrong, mate?"

He looked at me with big eyes. "It impossible. Cannot be."

"What? What is impossible?"

"You see lake?"

I glanced down at it. It was the shape of a half circle surrounded by lush greenery. There were a few buildings along the shore but I couldn't tell what they were from here. There was a large city beyond it, which seemed strange.

"Now I understand," Lasha said. The wind blew and I shivered.

"What do you understand?" I snapped.

He met my eyes and spoke in a voice tinged with awe and dawning understanding. "In 2005, there was incident here. You cannot find nothing about it now. SUS and CIA and FSB clean everything, every record, every trace. But in 2005, like I say, something was found here. Artifact. Treasure. Something like this. Russia and USA do everything they can to hide it. Only a few remember it now. Even our government maybe not know."

"Urban legend, mate," Dante said, not unkindly.

"Not legend. I know. I was here. On crew. I only one left alive."

"Okay," I said, not wanting to contradict him. "So where are we?"

He shook his head again. "That is fucked part. This Turtle Lake. We are in Tbilisi."

"Can't be," Dante said. "I could really use a drink."

"Impossible," I said at the same time. But I saw the city with my own eyes. "That's 200 kilometers away."

Lasha had dealt with his shock and had become philosophical about it. "Man come back from dead, maybe nothing strange."

"Good point," I said.

"Me?" Dante said. "What is this bit? It's not funny. I wasn't ever dead."

"Regardless of what Lazarus over here says," I said, "we need to get the hell out of the city. Lasha, can you get us to a safe place? I need to read more of this book. But first a shower. And a nap. Or maybe a nap and a shower. Either way."

"Let us hike down to lake. I can use phone," Lasha said.

"Mate, I really wasn't dead. I think I would know if I had been dead," Dante protested. I looked behind him and was only a little surprised to see there was no visible cave entrance where we had emerged from.

39

Ah, Yerevan: the city that looks like it was dipped in rosé and left to dry in the sun. The locals call it the "Pink City" because of the volcanic tuff stone used in the buildings, giving everything a charming, slightly faded, Soviet-chic glow. It's like someone took a Brutalist city and said, "Let's make it fabulous." Walk around Republic Square at sunset, and the whole place turns a shade of bubblegum pink that's almost enough to make you forget the chaotic traffic and the occasional death-wish Lada swerving past you. Almost.

Then there's the Hrazdan Gorge, which slices through the city like some sort of dramatic geographic afterthought. On one side, you've got high-rise apartments and fancy cafés where young Armenians sip espresso and scroll Instagram. On the other, there's a steep drop into a gorge that looks like it belongs in a nature documentary, complete with rusting Soviet-era infrastructure clinging to the cliffs. You can take a scenic stroll through the canyon, if you don't mind the occasional abandoned structure teeming with ghosts from the past.

But despite its quirks (and the occasional lungful of Soviet-era car exhaust,) Yerevan has a rough-around-the-edges charm. The people are warm, the brandy is smoother than you deserve, and the city somehow manages to balance ancient history with a distinctly post-Soviet identity. You can even climb the Cascade (a massive stairway/modern-art-installation) and be rewarded with a view of Mount Ararat, looming like an indifferent deity over the whole city.

Those are the words I wrote in my diary as I sat on my bed in Sun City Hostel, perhaps hoping I could convince myself I was just another traveler. This hunt had led me into deep waters. Strike that. All my adventures had led me to deep waters. This one had dropped me into the Mariana Trench. The world wide, there were no other waters so deep. I didn't like knowing that the Shepherds were still out there. But worse, I didn't like knowing the Golden Witch was behind them, whoever she really was.

Two days before, we had arrived back in Tbilisi. Just how we had was still a mystery. After we showered and then slept for a good ten hours, we had immediately set off for a Marshrutka, or intercity minibus, to Yerevan. It wasn't a long trip and I slept on that bus too, waking up only long enough to stumble through immigration and passport control. Mr Thupa had joined us with our gear and bags (including my much loved Macpac). Lasha decided to stay in Tbilisi even though we warned him how dangerous it would be. “It my city,” he said. “I stay.” I envied him that easy certainty, as well as connection to his country and culture. We said goodbye. He refused to take any money from me, but made no suggestion of returning the gun or sharing whatever he’d stuffed in his pack. I considered that a reasonable trade. He had come out of this whole affair alright indeed.

We had a flight to Tehran the next morning. I had read more of the book with the legend of the Golden Fleece. It was, at best, a highly unreliable guide but it was all we had to go on. And Dante’s presence was mute proof that it was not always wrong.

We were all staying in a cheap hostel. Some people think that just because I’m older and have some money, it is strange that I don’t do everything I can to avoid discomfort. I hate that. Discomfort makes us into people. It’s a crucial ingredient. You notice how old people are mostly arseholes and young people are mostly heaps chill? It’s all about being open to the world and not having expectations. Just as steel needs to be forged, so too does the human being. And it’s not like we were being tortured. Hostels are plenty comfy. You just have to remember how to exist in a space with people you don’t know.

***

Nephew here. I promise I don’t like coming in here, but there are an additional 17 pages of this rant on the ruin of society. This was one of the longest single sections of the book so it was clearly important to Uncle Jad. But it really is just a rant and you can find thousands of those wherever you go online. If you really want to read more of Uncle Jad’s thoughts about tempering people, email me and I’ll send you the section I cut.

***

Though I longed to explore the streets, we weren’t taking any chances. We stayed in and only left together to get food at the local supermarket. The local bread, lavash, was nearly as long as I am tall and no, mate, that’s not an exaggeration.

So we had enough food and we stayed together and chatted in low voices. Mr Thupa had caught us up on what had happened the nine days we had been gone. In a word, nothing. Once we had gone underground, so too had all the resistance we faced. I had also told him about our adventures. He had smiled like he didn’t quite believe me but didn’t want to contradict me. His man in Batumi was to join us in Iran.

There were twelve beds in the hostel room but we were the only three there. It was Friday night, after all. Everyone else was out enjoying the questionable nightlife pleasures of a weekend night in Yerevan.

Dante sat on the bottom bunk, I was cross-legged on the bottom bunk across from him and Mr Thupa had the top bunk above Dante.

"Tell me more about book," Mr Thupa said.

I hesitated. "A lot of this sounds pretty wild."

"In Nepal, we grow up reading Hindu and Buddhist texts. Believe me, nothing is wild after that."

"Okay. Well I told you about the mask of the Gold Witch." I shuddered at the memory of how much power had coursed through that cursed item. "It represented Hecate, the force behind Medea, the sorceress from the Argonaut tales."

"I know this stories," Mr Thupa said.

"Well, here's where it gets interesting. Medea is said after leaving Jason to have returned home, to what we now call Georgia, and then going on to the land of the Medes. Named after her, naturally."

"Iran," Dante clarified.

"Yes. Why she left the Fleece is conjecture but perhaps it's as simple as feeling bad that she stole it. Killed her brother to keep it. But as we saw, it hasn't sat idly. It's possible she's returned to it over the centuries. Kept herself alive."

"Okay, okay, hold on just one minute. You talk about Medea like she is some real person."

"I said it got weird."

"That's not being weird. That's making up stories."

"I know," I told him. "I'm not happy about it either. Do I really think there's some 3,000 year old crone tucked away somewhere in the remnants of the Persian Empire? Of course not. But could there be an ancestral position? Some powerful hidden figure with generational wealth and, more importantly, generational knowledge? That's not too hard to believe."

"You Nepalese believe in The Living Goddess anyway. How is some immortal witch different?" Dante asked.

Mr Thupa looked offended. "Kumari is something else. We shall not be discussing her here."

"Fair enough," Dante said. He was smart enough to know the futility of arguing something you don't care about with someone who was passionate about the other side of things.

"Maybe it's a corporation. Or a coven of witches. Whatever. We can safely say there is some kind of secret society that seems to have ties to the Golden Fleece. They are the ones who tried to stop us from getting to the treasure. They are the ones that tried to kill me. The ones who killed Nova. It's them we're going after."

"So much treasure," Mr Thupa said. "And it is all being left behind. Are you sure you're not going back?"

"No!" Dante and I said together. We looked at each other and began to laugh.

40

Another flight. Another landing. We met up with Mr Rai, the last of our Nepali soldiers. That led to another bus ride. All of this was handled by Mr Thupa as we assumed he was slightly less traceable than either of Dante or I, even using our myriad of fake IDs. It wasn't until Shiraz that I found out the problem.

It has been said that Shiraz is Iran's answer to the question, "What if an entire city was made out of poetry, flowers, and relentless traffic?" Nestled in the heart of Fars Province, the place had stunning gardens thriving in a desert, ancient history coexisting with belligerent motorbikes, and an air of cultural sophistication that somehow survived shopkeepers trying to sell you the same Persian carpet three times a day. If you have heard of poets like Hafez and Saadi, well their tombs are now pilgrimage sites for Instagram influencers keen to dramatically read poetry out loud. The Persian gardens (Eram, Narenjestan, and so on) were perfectly manicured oases that make you feel like an extra in a historical drama, assuming you can ignore the relentless sound of honking from outside the gates. The scent of citrus blossoms filled the air, mingling with the occasional whiff of kebabs, because, let's be honest, Iran runs on kebabs. The Pink Mosque (Nasir al-Mulk) is another highlight, and by "highlight," I mean you'll spend half an hour waiting for someone to move so you can take a photo of its famous stained glass without an awkwardly placed selfie stick ruining the magic. And, of course, there's Persepolis, the grand ruins of the Achaemenid Empire just outside the city. It's where ancient kings once ruled, and now, it's where tourists attempt to climb things they absolutely should not be climbing. The sheer scale of the place is breathtaking: columns stretching toward the sky, intricate carvings depicting centuries-old victories, and the faint echo of a guide explaining for the hundredth time that no, Alexander the Great was not the good guy here. He actually got drunk one day and burned the whole thing down. This is up there with Turkey storing their gunpowder in the Acropolis for sheer wanton lack of respect. I've always said: don't move through a place, let a place move through you and this was a place where that happened effortlessly.

Shiraz, for all the heat and noise and traffic, wasn't the problem. The problem was I was dry. It started at the cash machine right outside our guesthouse. My card was blocked. That was odd but not unprecedented. Over the next hour, I would try seven different cards at twelve different cash machines and get the same message. What started off as not a big deal was now settling in as a major headache. I went back to Guesthouse Ana and told Dante. He frowned and reached into his bag of tricks. I left with him and forty minutes later, we returned glumly.

We had opted this time for a private room shared by the four of us. Mr Thupa was out gathering information and supplies. Mr Rai remained in the room at all times. He was our bodyguard, and he protected our treasures when we had to leave the room.

"Mate, some of this is crypto. Some of this is offshore. I barely know about all these accounts. No one else on earth should be able to."

"Home computer hacked?" Dante asked.

"Please. There's nothing on anything public," I said. "I can check on my phone with password and thumbprint and that's it."

"I was afraid of that. Same deal for me. So how much cash do we have?"

I had an idea but I rummaged through my bag and then, after a nod of allowance, Dante's. I counted it twice.

"Could be worse," I said. "We have about 5,000 dollars in cash."

"Almost 3,000 euros," Dante said.

"Not nothing but it's a good thing we travel on the cheap."

"I assume once we meet these fellas on the other end, we'll be able to solve this problem."

"I think so," I said. Losing access to my wealth was horrible but somehow I was taking it well. Perhaps I was in shock or just couldn't believe it.

"You say you have no money," Mr Rai said. I was so unprepared for him to contribute to the conversation that he had to ask the question again.

"It's not a problem, mate. Just a glitch."

"What is glitch?" he asked.

"Just a setback. No worries."

"No worries," he said. He did not sound convinced. That was a problem for later and one that I promptly forgot about as Dante started shivering.

"Mate, it's 36 degrees out there. Are you ill?"

He shook his head. "Not ill. Just I have been feeling cold ever since … ever since we got back to Tbilisi."

"We could buy a jacket," I said. But he was the wrong size for this country even if we could find a place that sold ski jackets.

"I'll be fine," he said.

I looked around the room and had a genius idea. Not my first, you'll note, but it would turn out to be one of my best.

"Take off your shirt," I told him as I walked over to our bags.

"I'm cold, mate. Not randy."

"I know, I know. Trust me."

He did as I asked. I only went and pulled out the Golden Fleece and wrapped it around his torso. Despite its thickness, it fit him well as I wrapped it around three times.

"Not so tight," Dante said.

"Sorry." I loosened it a bit and then handed him back a blue flannel. He buttoned it up and zipped up his windbreaker. "I feel good," he said.

He looked a little bulky but with his large frame and muscles it just seemed like he had gained some mass. He stopped shivering almost immediately. The best thing was that we now had our most valuable possession with us. I checked to see if the map was still in its inner pocket of my jacket (it was) and the flame book in the outer pocket (it was as well).

"Okay, so, if we need money, what can we do?" I asked Dante.

"Outside of North Korea and Turkmenistan, this might be the worst place. All the sanctions against Iran make for a closed economy."

"Yeah, that's what I thought." We had a million tricks to make money, but none of them had been calibrated for closed economies. That was something to amend in the future, if there was going to be a future. The image of a golden face loomed up in my memory.

The panic hit me then. I could feel my heart beating rapidly, I was sweating like a dirty dog, and I felt nauseous and dizzy. "Get me ice," I said, to anyone who would listen. I promise, I'm not usually a panic attack guy but these were exceptional circumstances.

I tried to practice my breathing but the dizziness intensified. It was like spinning around and around and around and then stopping suddenly and trying to focus enough to read Shakespeare. Dante, bless his heart, was back before I realized he had gone. He knew what to do and placed the ice pack on my chest. The cold seeped into me with a burning intensity but I instantly felt better. Hot tip: placing an ice pack on your chest can stimulate your vagus nerve and immediately relieve the need to throw up in cases of motion sickness, panic attacks, or medication nausea.

I breathed deeply a few more times and felt close to normal. Then I looked around the room. "Where did Mr Rai go?" I asked.

Dante looked around and frowned. "Didn't notice him leaving." Dante saying that was both an admission of his own negligence and an admiration of the other's skill. Dante didn't miss much.

We waited for him for an hour. Then another. By that evening, when neither he nor Mr Thupa had returned, I knew we were boned.

41

We left our guesthouse at midnight and caught a cab to Narenjestan Garden. We didn't know if maybe something had happened to the Nepalese men, or if they had decided to leave us, or if they had gone over to our enemies. It said something that our best option was that something bad had happened to them. We had to assume that it was the worst, and that they had gone over to the enemy with all of our secrets. For all my paranoid fears, I somehow hadn't considered this happenstance.

The taxi dropped us off and we found what was called a Restaurant Garden that was open all hours of the night. The restaurant stretched over a huge area, with separate gazebos at different levels. The entire location was covered by lush greenery, and along the paths between the gazebos were rain waterfalls and canals. We hired an entire gazebo for ourselves and lugged our heavy tucker bags in (remember, we were carrying our cassowary shields among other things) and ordered some food and coffee. They seemed surprised and even slightly offended that we didn't want shisha, but I'm just not a smoker. Never have been. The hot food and coffee was served and we went to town. It was heaps tasty but I didn't feel better after eating most of it.

I gritted my teeth. It felt like a noose was around my neck, growing ever tighter. Dante seemed as unflappable as ever, but I hadn't forgotten what had happened to him. I had taken the loyalty of Mr Thupa and his men for granted. I needed to make sure I didn't do that again.

"Mate, how you going?"

It was a strange question in the circumstances and he didn't answer, only looked at me.

I began again. "What I mean is, can I get anything for you? Do you need something?"

"What are you on about?"

"I dunno, mate. Just want to make sure that I'm keeping you in the loop."

"Consider me looped," he said.

"If you need anything, you let me know."

"Is this about the Nepalese blokes? I'm not going to bail like that."

"I know you won't. But still. Tell me about any issues or problems you have, alright?"

"Yeah. You do the same."

"Deal. Now, keep watch for a minute, eh?" I asked. He nodded and I reached into my inner pocket and took out the book with a flame on the cover. It still burned with heatless flame, though it was almost invisible under the lights.

The section I turned to was written in old Avestan, the language of Zoroastrianism. (Actually that language didn't have an alphabet, as it was memorized without ever being written down, but later alphabets were added and I'll spare you the linguistic treatise to explain.) I could read it but it took a lot of concentration.

The first section was attributed to The Argonautica by Apollonius of Rhodes.

As the first light of dawn touched the sky, the maiden stirred. With swift, graceful hands, she gathered up her golden tresses, which tumbled about her shoulders in wild disarray. She bathed her tear-streaked face, smoothing her skin with an ointment sweet as nectar, and draped herself in a robe of surpassing beauty, fastened with well-wrought clasps. Over her head, radiant as the dawn itself, she cast a veil that shimmered like silver.

Through the halls of the palace she moved, her steps light yet her thoughts burdened, brushing aside the weight of her sorrows: sorrows sent by the gods, with yet more to come. She called out, and twelve maidens, as young and untouched by marriage as herself, stirred from their slumber in the perfumed vestibule of her chamber. She bid them yoke the mules, for she would journey at once to the shrine of Hecate, goddess of witchcraft and the crossroads.

Even as her attendants prepared the chariot, Medea reached for a treasure hidden within a hollow casket: the fabled charm of Prometheus. It was said that those who anointed themselves with its sacred essence, after offering midnight sacrifice to the Maiden of the Underworld, would be impervious to bronze and unshaken by fire. Born of a god's torment, the charm had first sprung from the ichor of Prometheus himself, spilled upon the crags of Caucasus by the eagle's cruel talons.

Far away, upon the sacred shores of the Phaeacians, Medea's fate would entwine with Jason's. There, beneath the vaults of an ancient cave, a great couch was spread, its splendor befitting legend. Upon it lay the Golden Fleece, its luster catching the flickering light, setting the chamber aglow like a living fire. Nymphs gathered from forest and river, their arms full of flowers, their voices hushed in reverence. Some came from the flowing streams of Aegaeus, others from the green crests of Meliteian hills, and still more from the shadowed groves of the plains. Hera herself, queen of the heavens, had sent them to honor the hero and his sorceress bride. To this day, the cave is known as the sacred dwelling of Medea, where fate wove its golden thread into legend.

There was more but having recently been in that exact cave, I felt justified in skipping ahead. I stopped when I saw a section written in Latin. It was an excerpt from Seneca's Medea which I scanned while I idly took a bite of the Sabzi Polo, a fluffy rice with saffron topping that was almost too incredible to describe. This was much easier to read.

With a whispered incantation, she called forth the entire tribe of serpents, their sinuous bodies writhing in answer to her dark summons. The air thickened with a venomous hush as she turned to her wicked hoard: an arsenal of cursed herbs and fatal flora gathered from the most forsaken corners of the world.

She had scoured the treacherous slopes of Eryx, where plants took root in barren rock and thrived in the breath of unrelenting winds. She had plucked twisted vines from the frozen peaks of the Caucasus, where Prometheus's blood had soaked the stones, and sought out the cruel poisons the rich Arabians smeared upon their arrows, the same deadly saps that dripped from the quivers of bold Medes and swift Parthian riders.

Farther still had she journeyed: beneath the cold skies of the northern wilds, where noble Sueban women harvested venomous secrets in the shadowed Hyrcanian groves. No season was beyond her reach. In the tender green of spring and the bitter grip of winter alike, she gathered her harvest: blossoms that promised death with their wicked bloom, roots twisted with the promise of an agonizing end.

With careful hands, she laid them before her. Each leaf, each petal, each drop of darkened sap pulsed with ancient malice. The time had come to weave their power into a spell unlike any the world had seen.

I felt like I had the idea. I thumbed through the next couple of pages quickly, seeing a reference from Herodotus, who mentioned the tradition that Medea fled to the land of the Medes after her time in Greece. He suggested that the Medes were named after her, as her influence shaped their culture. Diodorus Siculus recounted something similar. The Roman historian Justin, summarizing earlier accounts, described Medea's flight to the Medes and her son's eventual rule. Even the geographer Strabo got into the act, briefly mentioning the idea that Medea and her descendants played a role in shaping the Medean people. These I had all known. It was why we had come.

But it was the work of Timonax of Knidos, a Greek explorer at the Persian court, who wrote about Persian history and court life, that mentioned Persepolis indirectly. His works survive only in later summaries, so this discovery was a treasure in itself.

It is said that among the many wonders of Persepolis, beyond its gilded halls and towering columns, there lived a woman of terrible power, a sorceress whose presence unnerved even the Great Kings of Persia. The Greeks call her neat-ankled Medea, the daughter of Aeëtes, though the Medes knew her by another name: the Queen of Shadows.

When she fled from Corinth, scorned and betrayed, she wandered eastward, through the barren lands of the Bactrians and the rugged mountains of the Caspians, until she came to the royal court of the Medes. There, it is said, she wove her spells over their kings, whispering counsel in their ears, teaching them the secrets of fire and death. Some claim it was her son, whom some called Medus and some called Polyxenus, that ruled after her, but others (those who speak in hushed voices) insist that she never died at all. That her magic bound her to Persepolis, lingering through the reigns of Darius and Xerxes, hiding behind veils of illusion, waiting for the day when the Greeks would come. Swearing her vengeance upon the descendants of he who had wronged her.

When Alexander, son of Philip, entered the city in triumph, he did not find only gold and silk, nor the revelries of a fallen court. He found Persepolis darkened by unseen forces, its halls filled with whispers that did not cease, even when no tongue moved. His men spoke of visions, of ghostly figures flickering at the edges of the torchlight, of a woman's voice: low, commanding, and filled with laughter that chilled the blood.

On the night of the great fire, it was not wine and revelry that led the Macedonian king to his act of destruction. No, the truth is far stranger. He saw her: a figure wreathed in shadow and flame, standing upon the high terrace of the palace, her hands raised to the heavens. The fire did not consume her, nor did she flee. Instead, she watched as the city burned, as if welcoming the destruction. Some say it was Alexander's own fear that drove him to raze Persepolis to the ground, believing that only by turning its splendor to ash could he unmake the sorcery that dwelled within.

Yet, others whisper that Medea was never truly destroyed. That even now, her spirit lingers where Persepolis once stood, among the broken stones and scorched columns, waiting once more for an empire to rise, and for her vengeance to be obtained.

"What's it say?" Dante asked after some time.

I considered it for a minute. It was a lot to sum up. "Well, it seems as though some flowers grew from Prometheus's blood and they could be used for magic. One day, a sheep wandered up and ate them. He then became the golden ram, or golden fleece. There's a charm of Prometheus that protects against fire or maybe death. Medea based an empire in

Persepolis and Alexander burnt it down trying to get rid of her. Also, she had neat ankles."

"What?"

"I don't know. Maybe my Greek is rusty."

"Did you read it all?"

"Oh no. There's much more. Some in languages I don't even recognize."

"Do you want to read more now?"

There would be time for that later. "I reckon we have to get to Persepolis. We can catch a cab as soon as it's light. Let's try to get some shut eye." There were plenty of cushions, enough for both of us to make beds, and it had been a long day.

His nod of assent turned into a barely disguised grimace mid nod. "Might have a snack first," he said. "Thinking about trying the rutabaga."

I did not respond to his words but it took effort to hide my alarm. You'll recall that mention of a root vegetable was one of our emergency codes. I saw them now too, looming in the darkness outside our gazebo. Dozens of men dressed in rough homespun, with vests and little hats.

"How do they find us everywhere we go?" I asked.

"I don't know, but I reckon we get out of here and give them another chance."

"Do you have anything there that could distract them?" Even as I asked this, several men began to gather by the door.

"Look at the sides," he said. "They're just plastic. I'll hold them at the door and you get out the side. I'll join you."

This was the kind of haphazard shenanigans we'd committed to a dozen times, so he looked a little surprised when I said, "No."

"Eh?"

"No, mate. We go out together."

I could see on his face that he wanted to argue, but something held him back.

"Alright. On three?"

The door opened and the men came in before we could begin our count.

"Three!" I said and we scooped up our bags and ran toward the side. We heard shouts but no gunfire. We reached the side and saw that it wasn't plastic on the walls but glass. There were large gaps at the bottom revealing the garden on the other side.

I slung my pack down. "We can crawl through."

Dante followed suit. It was a tight squeeze, especially for him, but we were, let's say, motivated. I reached back in for my backpack only to have my hand grasped by a firm grip.

"Don't move," a harsh voice said. I was on my belly but managed to whip my hand out and away from him. Dante and I crawled away.

"Our bags," he said. "Everything."

"My Macpac is gone too. But at least we'll have a lighter load."

We had to get up and run then because the Shepherds had come around the gazebo.

We ran out of the garden and a Mazda pulled up. Was it strange to see a brown, Japanese car here? Yes, indeed, but far from the strangest thing that day. The passenger door swung open and a young man yelled at us, "Get in." Dante and I exchanged a look. Well, what did we have to lose?

We hopped in. "You going all the way to Persepolis, mate?"

The driver turned around and smiled, revealing perfectly white teeth. "Of course. Mother is very anxious to meet you both."

42

We drove out of the city and into the night. Leaving Shiraz, we traveled north on a well-paved highway, passing through the strikingly arid landscapes of Fars Province. The terrain was a mix of rugged hills, open plains, and scattered farmland, with occasional clusters of cypress and almond trees. The dark of night was just becoming slightly purple with the initial bloom of dawn when we drew close.

As we got closer to Persepolis, the land flattened out, and we saw low mountains in the distance. The entrance to the ancient site was well-marked, and even before we arrived, the monumental ruins came into view, giving a sense of the grandeur that awaited. No words had been exchanged the entire drive. It was almost as if all of us were afraid to break the silence: a standoff of sound too delicate to be broken. I had my suspicions of who his mother was but I dared not ask, in case he should answer me.

Finally the pressure of the silence got to me. "How you going, Dante?" I asked.

He shrugged. "Whelmed."

"Yeah, same."

The smiley young man stopped the car in a large, empty parking lot about a kilometer away from the entrance to the monument.

He stepped out of the car and lit up a smoke. I took a good look at him for the first time. He had short curly hair and a similar beard. He looked somewhat like a young Cat Stevens. When we emerged from the back seat, he greeted us with a smile so warm it almost dissolved the chill of the morning.

"We made it. I bet you have some questions for me, don't you?"

"Are we safe?" Dante asked before I could say anything.

The man laughed. "Definitely not. But you are safe from me."

I couldn't resist anymore. "You said you're taking us to your mother. Just who is she?"

"Yeah I thought you might want to know that. She's Medea, of course. Now hold on."

Dante immediately advanced upon him. "She just wants to talk," the boy said. He was so calm as he stuck out his hand, "I'm Paul, by the way. Paul E Zenus."

"Dante Merriweather," Dante said, shifting from aggression to handshaking in the blink of an eye, shaking his hand.

I stepped up and shook his hand too. "Jad Malek. Pleasure, mate."

"Agreed. Now let's get away from out in the open. The Raven could be anywhere."

"Who's that?" I asked.

For the first time since we'd met him, Paul looked surprised and unhappy, like when you realize that that unpleasant smell you keep smelling is dog poo that you stepped in without realizing. "You don't know? How did you survive this long? Perhaps we misjudged you."

I quickly put two and two together. "The assassin. I thought he was working for your mum."

"He kind of is. That's the problem. Come, we will explain more." The ruins were behind him and they sprawled, mate. It was a much bigger area than I'd imagined. A sad camel was being tied to a post near the entrance by a few of the touts that worked there as we walked away, but even that didn't take away from the ancient grandeur of the place.

We followed him, away from the ruins and toward a squat, brutalist building that looked like a defunct hotel. There were empty, sandy pits where swimming pools had once been. The door had been barred on the inside but Paul gave a strange low whistle and it opened immediately.

"Come in, come in," he said, beckoning us with his free hand. With the other, he finished his smoke and threw it on the ground. Persians were big smokers. I guessed it was the only real vice left to you when grog and sex were forbidden.

As we passed through the door, I felt very cold and very sad, but just for half a second. Dante shivered as well. I looked around to see if there were any people who could have opened the door, but we seemed to be alone. Paul stood in front of us, looking a little nervous.

"My mother, she's great. You'll love her. But she is a bit odd. Try not to piss her off, okay?"

"I'll try," I said, coughing suddenly.

The air was thick with perfume and cigarette smoke, though the foyer was empty. We walked through the grand lobby, hearing only the occasional creak of the ceiling fan as it feebly struggled against the desert heat. The marble floors were cracked, their shine dulled by decades of dust and neglect. The walls, once adorned with lavish Persian rugs, now bore only ghostly outlines where they used to hang.

There was a rotary phone sitting on a plastic chair next to a closet. For some reason, I didn't like that. It made me feel on edge. But we moved past it quickly enough.

We entered the first room on the right and stepped into … something strange. From outside, it looked like the grotty, grungy room it was. But inside, it felt almost like wearing VR. It was like being in two places at once. I could see the hotel room. But I could feel the cool, clean air of a high desert. In the distance, I could hear the sounds of another world, an ancient world, from far off.

A woman in a sharply tailored suit, a pristine cut in midnight black, approached. She had a serpent-shaped bracelet coiled around her wrist and her nails were immaculate, blood-red, and tapping rhythmically on her side. Her dark hair was fashionably short and spiky, like a star in an 80's music video. She looked like the kind of woman who only ever ordered Aperol spritzes, no matter the time of day or year, and when she spoke, it was in measured tones, each word laced with calculated persuasion.

"Gentlemen, greetings. You've come a long way, through great hardship. I salute you."

I couldn't help myself. "Hey, Medea. Neat ankles."

She looked surprised at that, then suppressed a laugh. "Ah, so you know your Hesiod. I might have known."

Such was the power of her charm that I felt flush with self-satisfaction, like a student praised by a stern teacher. Usually it was I that flattered for favor, but next to her I was an amateur. I felt myself blushing.

"Th-thank you," I said, stumbling over my words.

Dante seemed to sense the web I was caught in and he sliced it neatly in two with a simple comment. He stood next to me, a few paces into the room. Paul remained by the door.

"We need some answers from you," he said.

She laughed and it was the sound of diamonds sparkling. By the gods, she was a woman.

Medea glided across the room, her movements precise, each step purposeful. "I expected nothing less," she said, gesturing toward a low table set with a silver tray. On it, three small glasses of dark tea steamed, the scent rich with cardamom and something more elusive, something almost metallic. She picked up one of the glasses and held it between her fingers, watching us over the rim. "But the real question is, do you want answers? Or do you want the truth?"

Dante frowned. "Aren't they the same thing?"

Medea took a slow sip before setting the glass back down. "Not now. Not here. Not in this world." She turned to Paul, who had taken up a lazy stance by the doorway, his arms crossed. "Did you tell them about The Raven?" She handed each of us a cup of steaming tea. I took a moment, but then drank mine. They had us in their power. Dante apparently reached the same conclusion and drank his as well. Medea finished her cup as well.

Paul hesitated, then nodded. "Some. Enough."

"Not enough," Medea corrected. Her voice sharpened like a blade being drawn across a whetstone. "If they don't know what's coming, they won't last the day. I can't save them like I did with the monkeys in the airport. Not this time."

"That was you?" I asked. "But you've been trying to stop me."

"Oh no," she said. "I've guided your path when I could. In Kathmandu. In Pakistan, when I tried to keep you off the bus that was watched. In Yerevan when I pulled The Raven away from you. But my power is not the match of *hers*. Truly, I am a shadow of her. I'm truly sorry about your friend."

The room was warm, but I suddenly felt cold again, like that moment at the entrance of the hotel. Dante shifted uncomfortably, and I could tell he was feeling it too.

"Then tell us," I said, forcing my voice to stay steady. "Tell us what about The Raven. Truth or answers, doesn't matter."

Medea ignored him and studied me for a long breath. Then she smiled, but it wasn't a friendly smile. It was the smile of a cat that had just noticed a three-legged mouse. "Very well," she said. "Let's start with the most important thing: he's already here."

There was a sound from the hallway. A single, deliberate knock.

Paul moved before any of us could react. He threw the bolt on the door, his fingers steady despite the tension that suddenly thickened the air. No one spoke.

The calm knock came again. It wasn't the frantic pounding of someone desperate to be let in, nor the menacing hammer of a threat. It was worse. It was polite. It was confident. It was inevitable. It terrorized us with its patience.

Medea exhaled slowly, adjusting the serpent bracelet on her wrist. "Jad," she said without looking at me. "Would you be so kind as to pour me another cup of tea?"

I swallowed hard. "Now?" The smell of cardamom was strong in the air, overwhelming the distant scents of the past. Indeed, the impression of being in two worlds at once faded and disappeared.

She turned, her blood-red nails tapping against the silver tray. "Yes. Now." Her voice had the ring of peevish authority.

Dante shifted closer to me, his voice barely above a whisper. "She's stalling."

"Or preparing," I muttered back. My hand hovered over the teapot, but I kept my eyes on the door. Another knock. Still measured. Still waiting.

Medea finally straightened, smoothing the front of her suit as if she were about to take the stage. "Let's not have this go on forever, shall we?" And with that, she stepped forward and reached for the door.

43

I thought she was about to open it, but I was wrong. She reached for the lock but did not unlock it. Instead she traced a sigil that glowed with the faint moonlight of a forlorn autumn evening on the door handle. This only took a few moments and all of us watched in fascination as she did so.

As she finished, she rubbed her hands together with satisfaction. "That will keep him out. The Raven is powerful but cannot counter my magic." She turned to me and held out her slim hand.

"And now, if you don't mind, my tea and then the map please."

The map! With all that had happened, I almost forgot I still had it.

I reached into my inner pocket and pulled it out. But I hesitated. Not because I wanted to keep it, but its value was questionable now.

"We know where the entrance is. What good is the map?" I almost added, but didn't, the fact that we had looted the Fleece and the Book made the map even more redundant.

"Just a precaution," she said. "Others could find it," she said. Her tone was so casual that it alarmed me. But I didn't give any sign of my suspicion. I couldn't have said no to her anyway. Her charm overwhelmed me and I gleefully drowned in it.

But first I handed her a cup of tea. She smiled with grace. She then sat down and took a long drink of her cooling tea. She would get the map from me. It was a matter of time.

"How was the Fleece still there?" I asked. "Why didn't the Soviets want it? Why didn't you want it?"

She smiled politely. "I do want it. But it was there because that is where it belongs."

"And everyone just knew that?"

Her smile grew larger. "We let them know, if they didn't."

That sounded ominous so I changed the subject.

"Okay, fair enough. So who is this Raven?" I asked.

Her frown was slight but spoke volumes. "We call him Raven because he creates a murder whenever he intersects with other people. He's an arrow that once shot, cannot be recalled."

"Even by the one that shot it?" Dante asked.

"Especially by the one that shot it," she said. "But I didn't hire him, not in that sense. He cannot be killed. Cannot be stopped. He does what he does to impress me. To make amends. I cannot lie. I have used his services over the years. When the map was stolen, he went after it. I didn't mind at first. The thief was … a greedy little man. We weren't able to locate him but Raven removed his partner only hours after he sold the map to you. But once others got involved, it was beyond my control."

Some of that made sense, if she could be believed. That was only the beginning of our conversation but then, without any warning, the door opened.

Medea barely even had time to be surprised before she slumped to the ground. Only then, seeing her body crumple, did I process that a bullet had been fired.

"Jesus Christ!" I yelled.

A slim figure with broad shoulders walked in the door. In his right hand was a big Desert Eagle. There was something horrible in his left hand but my brain glitched over it, refused to process the scene before me. It was hard to look at that figure. It seemed to exist in a space that my mind skipped over. But also it looked familiar. I thought of an American baseball cap for some reason, and heard the sound of a distant, receding motorcycle.

"Gods," Dante hissed. He had processed the scene more quickly than I could. "So that's what happened to them."

And then I knew what I saw. Hanging by their hair were the heads of Mr Thupa and Mr Rai. They had been decapitated and their heads desecrated; their expressions showed great pain. *Better to die than live a coward.*

I don't get angry much: I'm a chilled out guy. But this sight filled me with a fury unlike anything I've ever felt. Up until this point in my life, I thought that "seeing red" was just a poetic way of describing rage. But I saw not just red but crimson, scarlet, carmine, and other shades I couldn't even name. I actually was crying tears of rage.

"You absolute dickhead," I said. I threw myself at the man holding the heads even as I processed what he himself looked like. He was visibly long dead. His face was rotten and feral, a snarling fester of soggy, cruel features. His lean body was a brown-green hue and smelled like it had been buried in the earth for months. I leapt and hit him with all my force, shoulder to his chest. It was, I don't mind saying, a terrifically powerful strike. It would have knocked Dante down, would have floored someone even bigger than Dante.

But it was like hitting a rock. It was I that ended up on the floor, bouncing off his chest like a rubber ball. Dante advanced upon him too, more cautiously, more cunningly, more craftily. He ended up on the floor next to me, seconds later. We lay there, gathering our breath. I could see, several meters away, the motionless body of Medea.

Paul watched all of this with an unreadable expression.

"You're still an asshole, Raven, or whatever you're calling yourself these days," he said.

The monstrosity threw the heads *at us*. Dante and I both scrambled up to avoid the heads and they both hit the ground where we had lain. I almost attacked him again but Paul spoke, forestalling me.

"That's actually a compliment. He very rarely takes trophies. It means they impressed him."

The Raven creature spoke, in what seemed to me to be a series of groans and hisses, but Paul listened intently.

"Ah. He says that they would not talk. Would not give you up. Even under great pain. Immense pain, rather. He kept their heads as a sign of respect."

"You can talk to it?" Dante asked. "You understand it?"

Paul looked embarrassed. "Well, I ought to. He used to be my father."

44

The silence that followed was as thick and oppressive as an old jar of vegemite. Even the air itself seemed to recoil from Paul's admission. My mind struggled to process it. Paul was claiming this grotesque revenant as his father?

Dante and I exchanged a glance, neither of us quite knowing what to say. Medea remained motionless on the floor, a dark pool seeping outward beneath her. I couldn't tell if it was tea or blood. The Raven, or whatever was left of him, stood utterly still, his mildewed form framed by the doorway like some awful sentry from a nightmare.

"You're serious?" I finally managed. "That thing used to be your dad?"

Paul exhaled sharply. "Not used to be. Still is." He turned to face the creature, his eyes scanning its ruined features as if looking for something familiar. "It wasn't always like this. He wasn't always like this. It's complicated."

The Raven tilted its head slightly, watching Paul with a strange, unreadable intensity. Then, it spoke again, if you could call it that. The noises that came from its throat were an abomination, the rasping of dead lungs forced to function long after they should have ceased. Paul, to my increasing horror, nodded along as if this was the most natural conversation in the world.

"Okay," Paul said. "I'll tell them." He turned to us. "Not many know this, or have ever been allowed to know this. But he wants you to know, before … well he wants you to know. He was once known as Jason, the hero of Thessaly. He was the leader of the Argonauts. His time with the Fleece changed him and left him deathless."

I had an uneasy feeling. In my experience, information was expensive. Someone who gave it away had a reasonable expectation that it couldn't be used against them. That said, Dante and I could shout all we wanted about a zombie assassin who was Jason from Greek Legend and it wouldn't exactly convince a reasonable person. Maybe a few Yanks, but that's the best case scenario. But still, I was cautious.

"Does the Fleece affect everyone like that?" I asked.

Dante looked uncomfortable. He hated this woo nonsense.

"Oh no. He was cursed by Medea with the same spell used on the skeleton warriors who once guarded the Fleece."

"So what does he want?" It felt weird to talk about the bloke right in front of him, but I wasn't going to stare at his zombie face if I could help it.

Paul crossed his arms and leaned back against the wall. "He's been trying to get back the favor of Mother for thousands of years. Sometimes she ignores him for a few centuries. But when she needs someone or something, there's no one better in her network."

"And so he shot her?"

Paul shrugged. "Like I said. It's complicated. It wasn't for her. It was for *her*."

"My money," I said. "She cut me off. How, and why?"

"I would guess to encourage you to come to her. But don't worry about that."

"Well, mate, I am just a little worried about that. I've had my house tossed, my friends killed, my money stolen, been shot at, knocked off a cliff, and had giant freaking spiders trying to eat me. Yeah I'm just a bit worried about it all."

"You should know that the Shepherds have sworn to kill you both. Don't worry. I can protect you."

I wanted to ask at what price, but the eighth rule of tomb raiding is: when negotiating, delay establishing the price for as long as possible.

"What is the deal with them?" I asked.

"They are a cult that worship Raven. Many of his so-called hits are actually done by them. In your case, he personally came after you in Australia, in Pakistan, in Nepal, in Armenia. They are based in Georgia, for obvious reasons."

"You're okay with him killing your Mum?" Dante asked.

"Not really," Paul said. We all looked over the undead monster that remained in the doorway. How fast could it raise its gun? I wondered. I suspected that the answer was: much faster than I wanted. "But it wasn't the first time. Now I can deal with him. But I need you to hand over the map."

I opened my mouth and closed it. He sensed my hesitation. "Come, both of you. Walk with me. Raven, come with us."

We walked out of the dim, cardamom scented room, and back into the hallway and out into the world again. Before us stretched a city of stone and gold: Persepolis, but not the ruins we had known. This was Persepolis alive. Before, it had felt like we were half in the modern world, half somewhere else. Now we had travelled to another world. It felt like being on a movie set, except this was no artificial construction. This was real.

We walked through the Gate of All Nations, its towering lamassu casting long shadows over the polished stone. The walls, no longer bare ruins, shone with vibrant paintings: scenes of tribute-bearers from across the empire, each detail as crisp as if it had been painted yesterday. The Apadana loomed ahead, its massive columns stretching toward the sky, capped with elaborate capitals shaped like twin-headed bulls. I swallowed hard, trying to process what I was seeing. It wasn't just the architecture, it was the sheer weight of history pressing down on me.

The air shimmered with heat, carrying the mingling scents of roasting meat, exotic spices, and something floral: myrrh, maybe, or storax. The aroma of a great empire at its peak. My stomach twisted at the sheer reality of it all. This was no illusion. This was time itself unraveled before our eyes.

Dante turned to Paul, his expression unreadable. "Is this real?"

Paul smiled. "As real as anything. Truth or answers." He gestured ahead. "Come on. Let's keep moving."

We followed, threading through the broad avenue, past nobles in embroidered robes and servants bearing trays of pomegranates and wine. The sound of voices rose and fell around us, a dozen languages spoken in a steady hum, punctuated by the bray of camels and the distant strains of lyres from some unseen courtyard.

I nearly stumbled as we passed a line of soldiers in shining bronze armor, their spears held at precise angles. Their eyes flicked over us but did not linger. It was as if we belonged, as if we were just another part of the great tide of people moving through the city.

"I don't like this," I muttered. "This isn't just some vision. We're really here, aren't we?"

Paul glanced at me, his expression unreadable. "That depends on your definition of 'here.'"

I gritted my teeth. "That's not comforting."

Dante let out a low whistle, tilting his head back to take in the vastness of the city. "This is bloody incredible," he said, almost reverent. "But why bring us here?"

Paul didn't answer immediately. Instead, he slowed as we approached a grand staircase leading up to the great palace. At the top, beyond the colonnades and flickering torches, I could just make out the shadowy figure of someone waiting.

Paul turned to us. "Because she wants to see you."

"She?" I asked. I had a sour feeling in my stomach.

"Yeah, the actual Medea. The ancient one. Not that modern shadow, though she was not without power. This is the high priestess of the

Golden Witch. The Queen of the Shadows. Don't worry. I can protect you from her."

I knew then that the time had come to start negotiating.

45

By some part of the magic that had brought us here, no one noticed us, not even when we began to climb up some kind of ziggurat. There were armed guards on the sides and I wondered how much their armor would be worth if I could just bring some back.

Raven walked behind us, perhaps as an honor guard, perhaps to ensure that we didn't try to slip away. He looked alive here. More than alive. Heroic. Bronze was his skin and mighty were his thews. He saw me looking at him and he met my eye with a malign grace. Something about his face said "Just you wait." I wondered if he was planning on killing us. They had said that he couldn't be stopped, and he had broken through her magic, but that had been in our world. Perhaps different rules applied here. If so, what did that mean for my carefully constructed rules?

We were about halfway up the stairs, maybe fifty or sixty meters, when I could not restrain myself anymore.

"So, Paul, why is the map so important? And if it is, why not just kill us and take it?"

"That map is the key to everything. It was stolen from this time, from this place. It needs to be returned. We certainly would have killed you for it, but at this point it seems better to stop underestimating you. I guess you can say that you impressed us. When certain people demonstrate great skill, we prefer to bring them into the fold."

I knew what he was doing. He was buttering me up, trying to make me feel important. The problem was that he was bloody good at it.

"So the deal is that I give you the map, and you return my money to me. Have me sign some kind of NDA. Go back to my life."

He nodded. "Something like that. Medea will decide."

"I've heard that before. How many Medeas are we going to meet? How are this one's ankles?"

Dante chuckled. "You're a galah, mate."

Paul shook his head and said nothing.

We reached the top without saying anything else. Medea waited for us.

I guess I was expecting someone queenlike and grandiose. She had the same face as before, but she was wearing a simple dress and her curly hair didn't seem like it had been combed recently. She looked strikingly similar to Wuthering Heights era Kate Bush, looking ready to start twirling around at any second.

"Would you like some tea?" she asked.

"I'll pass," I said.

"Ah, now you're thinking maybe the tea you had earlier was laced with something. Well, I can't say that I blame you. It's that prudence which has brought you this far."

I hadn't been actually, but now that she said it I began to wonder: could all this be some mushroom or acid induced trip? I perhaps could not definitely say it wasn't, but it did not seem plausible. Dante came and stood next to me. Paul descended down the stairs about fifteen steps to have a quiet conversation with Jason.

She looked at the pair of them and for a moment her mask slipped. She didn't like them.

I saw behind her, for a moment. There was a red, rotary phone on a wooden bench. Instead of a traditional mirror or pool of water, there were high tech screens that seemed to be connected to vast data networks. For a moment, I saw thousands of live feeds from all over the world, all at once. That hurt my brain so badly that my nose began to leak blood and I looked away.

"It takes a lot of power and effort to keep you here. Let's get to it," she said.

"Yes, let's. How about this? You ask a question and we answer it, and then vice versa." I wiped away some of my nose blood with the sleeve of my shirt.

She scoffed, but somehow not rudely. "That's hardly fair. I know *much* more than you do."

"If you didn't want some answers, I would hardly be here, would I?"

"I suppose not. Very well, I'll answer your questions. But remember I'll give you answers, not truth."

I still didn't know the difference. I guessed living for a few thousand years would make anyone a bit odd.

"Wait. You know what the other one said?"

"Don't you know what your shadow does? That little fool. She thought she was helping you. All along she did my bidding."

I felt like she was trying to goad me so I ignored that. "My shadow doesn't really do anything."

She looked sad at that.

"Mine do. All of them. Will you answer me now?"

"Fine. You can go first," I said.

She did not hesitate. "Why won't you give me the map?"

"Why don't you just take it?"

"Ah, ah, ah. That's not an answer."

"True," I said. "I'm happy to give you the map. But I just want to know what use it is to you. You know where it goes. I know where it goes. Who cares about the map now?" My nose had mostly stopped bleeding now.

She chewed on her lip and muttered something in a language so ancient it even sounded dusty.

"You're acting like you don't know. The map is a piece from Hecate's own realm. Of course you need the map in your hands to open the security door. And you need the map to use the Fleece. That map is, in its own way, as valuable as any treasure in the world."

I thought back. I had put my hand on my heart both times. I hadn't touched the map, but apparently that little bit of jacket wasn't enough to stop the magic. That was interesting. But I could not stall any longer.

I reached into my pocket and withdrew it. "Here. Now tell me why you want it."

She hesitated, as if fearing some trap. Then she snatched it out of my hands and glanced at it briefly.

"I have it," she called. "You can kill them."

"Oi!" I objected. "And here I complimented your ankles and everything." This response might seem overly glib, considering the circumstances, but I was actually just that relieved that I finally knew where she stood.

Jason raised his gun. Dante tensed beside me, but we both knew the big man, quick as he was, was not faster than a speeding bullet.

"Wait," Paul said. "Mother, let them live." Ugh. This was such a rehearsed and yet still fully shithouse version of good cop/ bad cop.

"Just kill us," I said. "Save us the amateur theater hour."

"Yeah I thought ancient Greeks were supposed to be good at theater," Dante said, taking my lead. It surprised me and I laughed much harder than I should have.

The pair of them looked furious now. I suppose most people in their circle treated them with just a bit more respect. Me, I'm a man of principle. And that principle is: never respect anyone who is at their core an utter unpleasant person.

Paul tried again. "We don't have to be enemies. Tell us where the Fleece is."

Dante and I both worked very hard to give no reaction to this. Medea had known so much about us the whole time. How did she not know it was this close to her? I supposed it was a greater magic than even hers, that some part of Prometheus kept it hidden from her. And physically, there was no sign of it on Dante. He just looked like a big dude wearing a couple of layers.

The reason they had kept us alive made sense. They needed information from us. I slowly eased my way toward the stairs.

"You'll never find it," I said. "Let us go and I'll send the location on a postcard."

"That's cute," he said. I moved closer to the stairs. I looked down and could see Paul and Jason looking up at me.

"I just can't seem to remember," I said. "Maybe it was something I ate. I might be allergic to taro root." I didn't dare look back at Dante but I hoped this random insertion of a root vegetable would make him alert.

"Jad, no," he said softly.

Paul moved his hand to his eyes to cover the midday sun. From somewhere deep in the city, a bell began to toll. *How appropriate.* "Just tell us," Paul said. "If you play your cards right, you can end up with a lot of money."

"It's a pity I'm not much of a card player. But I know a hell of a fold, taught to me by a great friend."

I launched myself at the two of them. I knew I could knock them both down the stairs. The fall would surely kill me but them as well, if die they could. I just had to be faster than Jason and his deadly gun.

46

The last thing I felt was a bullet going through my brain.

EPILOGUE

That's really how it ends. I know, how could Uncle Jad write that? It made me wonder if any part of it was real. Perhaps he had died of cancer or something and wrote this adventure story to cheer himself up. I wanted to believe that, because otherwise the world was heaps worse than I had guessed. At any rate, I wanted Jad's life (fictional life perhaps) to be known to the world. That's why you are reading these words now.

It wasn't easy. I was turned down by one hundred and seventeen publishers. All writers are paranoid and when they don't find success they believe the world is out to get them. But in my case, it might actually have been true. I'm lucky and grateful that Severed Press has taken a chance on me and hope they are not in any danger. If there was a Medea, of course she would suppress this. I know, you might think that I had grown paranoid from reading this book too many times and doing all the research, but things began to disappear from my room. Out on the streets of Brisbane, where I live now, sometimes people just stand and watch me. I know that they want to know what I know.

***

Publisher's note. We had this book ready to publish for seven and a half months. The cover was commissioned, the book edited, and the release date scheduled. We just needed one more signature from the author, Ahimsa Kerp. But he stopped answering calls, emails bounced back, and he did not respond to our snail mail. To be honest, after three or four months, the manuscript was forgotten.

That all changed one sunny day in January. A beaten package arrived with about a dozen stamps affixed to the brown paper wrapping. It had come from Zanzibar and when Georgia the intern opened it, she brought it straight to me. I couldn't believe what I saw. There was the last page of the contract, signed at last. With it was a handwritten note from the author. A sticky note on the paper said "Sorry I'm late. I've been busy." We present that note here.

The night before I had to send my final edits back to the publisher, a miracle happened. As I came home from a midnight showing of Alan Qatermain, I was surprised when a figure emerged slowly out of a dark van and walked towards me. I wished I had pepper spray, but it was hard to get unless you lived out in woop woop.

I turned toward the dark figure as it came up on the pavement. I made a fist, perhaps the first of my life, and tried to look brave and strong.

"What do you want?" I said loudly but my voice was swallowed up by the vast silence of the neighborhood. "I believe you are in the wrong neighborhood."

"And I believe whatever doesn't kill you, simply makes you stranger." The voice was gruff but familiar.

I stared more closely. There was just enough streetlight to make out some features.

"Uncle Jad?"

"In the flesh." He performed a little bow and then came up to hug me. He was lean but hugged with the strength of a demon.

"It's good to see you, lad."

"But you're dead!"

"Can anyone with access to the Golden Fleece truly be said to be dead?"

"Wait, that's real? But don't you need the map?"

"Yeah, you do. Dante and I are even, let's put it that way."

"But you've been dead for years."

"The Queen of the Shadows has eyes everywhere. I had to wait until it was safe."

"And it's safe now?"

"Oh hell no. But it won't get safer for you anytime soon. I didn't realize how much danger you'd be in. Of course, you didn't have to go publish the bloody damn thing! Think of how many people have read it already?" He sounded mad but also proud. The guy loved getting his flowers, and who can blame him?

"But how do you know? The book isn't even out yet."

"Come with me," he said.

We walked toward the dark van. I looked around, expecting to see someone coming after us, but the street was empty.

"I have so many questions. Why did the Raven shoot Medea? If he had been trying to win back her favor for centuries, why betray her now? What did he want? How did you escape the liminal world? How did you get your money back? And why did—?"

He put his hand on my shoulder as we reached the door of the van. "In time, my lad, in time."

"Okay, but I have one more question for you."

"Is it important?"

"It is to me."

"Shoot."

"What was the fifth rule on the art of tomb raiding?"

His smile revealed pure delight. "Rule five? I'm going to meet Dante and another friend at the gates of hell in Turkmenistan. Come join us and I'll teach it to you."

"Are you serious?"

"Why else would I be here?"

"Was any of what I read real?" I asked.

He smiled playfully. "Well, I really wrote it. You can't dispute that."

"No, I guess I can't."

We slipped into his van and drove off into the night.

THE END

www.ingramcontent.com/pod-product-compliance
Lightning Source LLC
Chambersburg PA
CBHW072239190626
46809CB00018B/2850
* 9 7 8 1 9 2 3 1 6 5 6 0 1 *